ECHOES OF YESTERDAY

Vet Keira Forrest thought she'd seen the last of GP Daniel Grant after he callously dumped her best friend, but now she finds herself having to give him emergency first aid after an accident. Worse, her new job is right next door to his surgery and the local matchmakers are busy. She is determined to avoid him, but an engaging wolfhound puppy named Finn and a family of delinquent cats have other ideas.

Books by Rachael Croft
in the Linford Romance Library:

RACHAEL CROFT

ECHOES OF YESTERDAY

Complete and Unabridged

LINFORD
Leicester

First published in Great Britain in 2004

First Linford Edition
published 2005

British Library CIP Data

Croft, Rachael
    Echoes of yesterday.—Large print ed.—
Linford romance library
    1. Love stories
    2. Large type books
    I. Title
    823.9'14 [F]

    ISBN 1–84395–898–8

Published by
F. A. Thorpe (Publishing)
Anstey, Leicestershire

Set by Words & Graphics Ltd.
Anstey, Leicestershire
Printed and bound in Great Britain by
T. J. International Ltd., Padstow, Cornwall

This book is printed on acid-free paper

1

As soon as Keira heard the frenzied neighing of the terrified horse she was out of her car and racing up the cobbled street towards the sound. Her mind had switched from nervousness about the afternoon ahead, to an overwhelming desire to help.

There was no way she could sit in the traffic jam and do nothing. Thank heaven she'd opted for sensible flat shoes and trousers, rather than the smart interview suit and heels her mother had advised.

'Can you let me through, please? Excuse me — ' she said as she moved towards the crowd.

A slight figure, dark hair flying, she shouldered the bag she'd grabbed from the car and pushed her way through the small crowd.

Above the heads of the onlookers she

caught a glimpse of a plunging chestnut form foam-spattered, eyes rolling in terror. She increased her pace.

Thankfully people moved aside for her and she reached the front of the crowd, emerging breathlessly into a small market square. The horse seemed quieter now, a small man in a drab anorak was holding the bridle and speaking reassuringly to the frightened animal. Keira felt a wave of relief. Looked like there was no major harm done.

A harassed-looking young policeman spotted her and hurried over. 'Thank goodness — help at last! The ambulance is stuck in traffic on the bypass and they've no idea how long it'll take them to arrive.' His radio crackled but he ignored it. 'Anyway, he's over this way.'

Keira had started to move towards the horse, but she stopped short. 'Who is? What do you mean?'

'The casualty. He needs help fast.'

'But the horse — '

The policeman gave her an incredulous glance. 'The horse? Forget it, it's OK. Fred Parker's looking after it, and the vet's on his way.' He gestured towards a small group of people standing round something on the ground. 'There's an injured man here, and he looks in a bad state to me. Come on, Doc.'

Keira followed the direction of his pointing finger and her heart thudded. What she'd at first taken to be an old coat lying on the ground was in fact a man, lying ominously still on the cobblestones, a car rug hastily thrown over him. He wasn't moving. She hesitated half a second, then followed the policeman over.

'Hang on a minute,' she attempted, tugging at his sleeve. 'I'm not a doctor.'

'Doctor, nurse, what does it matter? I don't care if you're a midwife — you are medically qualified, I suppose, or you wouldn't have come forward?'

'Well, yes, but — '

3

'Then you must be able to do something.'

There was no arguing with that, or with the note of near panic in the young policeman's voice. Keira pushed a strand of hair out of her eyes and knelt down beside the injured man. His face was chalk-white against the cobble-stones, his eyes were closed, his breathing shallow.

She recognised him immediately, and her heart lurched against her ribs. Her mouth went dry.

'Oh surely not, it's Daniel Grant.'

'That's right — know him, do you?'

'You — you could say that. I knew him — slightly — at university.'

No point in adding that this was the man who ruined her best friend's life. All right it was five years ago, but some memories didn't fade. Keira tightened her lips as the past rose up again with startling clarity, summoned up by this dark-haired man who lay on the roadway like a crumpled rag doll.

Visions swam unprompted before her

eyes — Daniel — tall, dark, handsome and didn't he know it — Daniel and Miriam hand-in-hand crossing the campus, eyes only for each other. And then, months later, Miriam in hysterical tears clutching at Keira's hand while Daniel walked away without turning his head — herself, trying to comfort the distraught Miriam, listening to her sobbing that Daniel Grant was a complete swine and what she wouldn't do to him given the chance.

Now Keira had that chance. He was completely at her mercy.

She swallowed hard, making an effort to push away negative thoughts. 'What happened to him?'

The policeman knelt beside her. 'Looks bad, doesn't he? The horse went right over him. He was a hero — pushed a little girl out of the way, but he copped it himself. What's the damage?'

Keira took one long-fingered hand in her own, feeling for a pulse. It was rapid and erratic. She spoke to the policeman, but it was as much for her own benefit as his as she rapidly scanned Daniel Grant's symptoms, fighting to distance herself from the personality behind the accident victim. 'There's a contusion on the side of his head; it looks superficial but he's pretty groggy — probably concussed. I'm more worried about the damage to his chest, you say the horse went over him?'

'So they told me. I didn't see it.'

'Well, these ribs look to be at an odd angle. The veins in his neck are standing out, see, probably the blood vessels inside the chest are compressed. It's distended on this side — I'd say he's damaged a lung and it's leaking air into his chest cavity.'

'So what needs doing?'

'Reduce the pressure inside his chest and fast. How long did you say that ambulance would be?'

'Fifteen minutes, with luck. Will it wait?'

Keira bit her lip. No, it couldn't wait. Not fifteen minutes. She was going to have to treat this man — she'd never done it before, never would again. She wasn't qualified to carry out the procedure on him, and it could mean prosecution if things went wrong. Even if they went right.

But she couldn't sit and do nothing. Even in the short time she'd been kneeling here the bluish colour round Daniel's lips had worsened. She came to a decision. She had to do it. There was no choice.

'Pass me my bag, will you?' While the policeman went over for the bag she sat back on her knees and thought hard. There was just one last appeal to try. 'What about the local GP? Has anyone sent for him?'

And then Daniel's dark eyes flickered open, and despite the dullness of pain she could have sworn that wry amusement shone in the depths. 'Sorry to disappoint.' His voice was faint, but very steady. 'I am the local GP.' Then, with an apparent effort, he focussed on her face. 'Keira — Keira Forrest?

What's going on?' He grimaced. 'Hard to breath — '

'It's OK, don't worry. You've had an accident.' Keira pasted on what she hoped was a reassuring smile. So he remembered her after all this time. She wouldn't have expected it — in fact she would vastly have preferred him not to. She wondered whether to tell him what she was about to do, but decided against it. No point in adding a cardiac arrest to his other problems. Mercifully his eyes closed, and he seemed to drift back into unconsciousness. No time to waste.

She reached into the bag, willing her fingers not to shake, and opened a sterile packet containing a hollow needle and cannula. Too large really, not intended for quite this purpose, but it would have to do. 'Can you keep people back?' Her voice sharpened with tension. 'They're standing in my light.'

While the policeman urged the onlookers back to a reasonable distance she quickly unbuttoned Daniel's shirt.

She thought hard — fourth intercostals space, and — oh yes, there's an artery to avoid, and the intercostals nerve — I've got to get it along the upper border of the rib . . .

She probed along the skin, discoloured with bruising. No spare flesh there, thank heaven, the edge of the rib was easily felt. A quick once-over with an alcohol wipe — no local anaesthetic, it was going to hurt. She pushed the heavy needle home, praying that she had the right place. Air immediately flowed out through the cannula, and Keira closed her eyes in a brief moment of thankfulness. Then it was a moment's work to slide in a catheter and remove the needle.

'That's it, Doc?' The policeman was looking on with interest.

'Reckon so, for now. I'll just tape this down. I'd better check for other injuries.'

She carried out a routine examination, working on autopilot, checking from time to time that the catheter was still venting. Her fingers traced the firm outline of Daniel's body, down from the hipbone, along the well-muscled thighs, down over the shins and ankles. Everything seemed OK, looked like the damage was confined to his upper body. She glanced at the neat taping and could hardly believe what she'd done. It looked like it was going to be all right.

She leaned over and spoke to Daniel, taking his wrist in her fingers to check his pulse. 'Won't be long now, you'll soon be in the hospital.'

Again his eyes met hers, and his mouth moved, though she had to lean right down to catch the whispered, 'Thanks.' She felt the brief pressure of his long fingers, then his eyes closed again and he relaxed.

She stared down at him. Now the immediate danger was past she allowed herself the luxury of a lingering inventory, still incredulous that their lives could have intersected again. He hadn't changed, not really, though the lines round his eyes had deepened, and he was more tanned than she remembered, his jaw line more taut. His body was leaner, all hard-packed muscle and bone and there was the odd streak of silver in the dark hair that fell over his forehead. Gently she smoothed it back, very aware of her fingers trailing over his skin.

Remembered emotion came rocketing back and with a wry little smile she sat back on her heels, eyes unfocussed. Daniel Grant! Heart-throb of half the girls in the medical faculty, not to mention the vet school. He'd certainly had his fair share of admirers.

She'd not been immune herself, she made herself admit. But he'd overlooked the quiet, dark-haired Keira Forrest and gone for her medic friend, brash, outgoing Miriam Taylor. That had been a blow, but nothing compared to the way she'd felt when later he'd messed up Miriam's life so badly. Keira and her friends, outraged and full of sympathy for the distraught Miriam,

11

had vowed they'd never forgive him.

But now, seeing him so vulnerable, lying on the dusty cobbles, old feelings of tenderness stirred. You couldn't go on hating forever. Tentatively, holding her breath, she reached out a hand to touch his cheek.

Then somewhere behind her an ambulance siren blared and people moved aside to let the vehicle through. A green-clad paramedic squatted down beside Keira. 'How is he?'

She snapped back to reality. 'Stable I think. He'll need oxygen. Nothing to lower his blood pressure.' She briefly described what she'd done. 'Possible head injury, and keep an eye on that cannula as you lift him.'

The paramedic glanced at it. 'Good grief, I could hardly miss it. Where did you get hold of a thing that size?'

Keira said nothing. This wasn't the time for pointless explanations. Anyway, now that the emergency was over the full implications of what she'd just done were beginning to hit her, and it wasn't a pleasant train of thought. Had she been right to intervene? Could she be sued for what she'd done? Or prosecuted?

The paramedics took over and she left them to it. She got to her feet, abstractedly trying to brush the dust of the street off her knees. She felt dazed and anticlimactic. What to do now? Where was her car? She looked around for the horse, but someone had led it away.

The policeman was beside her again, calmer now. 'You did a great job there. I reckon you saved his life.'

Keira dredged up a smile. She just wanted to get away, forget the whole unreal episode. Come to terms with Daniel Grant's sudden reappearance in her life, decide how she was going to cope with it. 'Maybe,' she said to the policeman. 'But it was a routine enough procedure.'

'Right. Work in A and E, do you, Doc?'

'Not exactly.' Keira picked up her

bag. 'And I told you, I'm not a doctor.'

'Oh yeah, sorry. A nurse, then?'

Keira sighed. 'No.'

'What then?' The man's brow creased in a frown. 'I have to make a report. Are you an auxiliary? Physio? Dentist?'

'None of those.' Keira watched as the bemused expression on the young man's face turned to suspicion and distrust tinged with genuine alarm. Quite plainly he was beginning to think that she was some totally unqualified person who had turned up to play doctors. And he was responsible for letting her do it.

Feeling sorry for him, she took a deep breath. She couldn't let him agonise like this. 'Actually,' she said slowly, wanting to test his reaction, 'I'm a vet.'

The policeman's jaw dropped. He stared at her, his mouth working soundlessly. 'A — a — vet?' he managed at last. 'And you stuck that needle into his chest — ' One or two onlookers stared, someone laughed briefly.

'Well,' he managed at last. 'I'll have to take down a few details for my report.' He took out a notebook. 'Can you give me your full name?'

Keira obliged, patiently answering his questions, very aware that the poor constable was acutely embarrassed by the whole thing, and quite plainly was wondering if he would be hauled over the coals for allowing a vet to carry out such a procedure. She could sympathise with him.

As the interview was coming to an end, a plump girl with a notebook and pencil materialised at her side. 'Did I hear you say you were a vet?'

Keira nodded. She was beginning to feel increasingly fatalistic about all this.

'And you actually treated Doctor Grant?'

'I did, yes. I had suitable equipment with me, there were no other medical practitioners present. It was a life or death situation.'

'Well, I think it's fantastic,' the girl

breathed, scribbling furiously. 'I'm from the local paper, by the way, and I'd like a few details, if you don't mind. And a photo would be good — over here, Phil.'

Keira frowned. The last thing she wanted was to provide entertaining breakfast-time reading for the local citizens. And, oh heavens, a story like that might even make it into the national press. She had a sudden vision of Miriam reading it over her morning coffee, and shuddered.

She started to frame excuses. 'It's no big deal. I'd rather just leave it.'

'Oh, please! Doctor Grant is so popular round here — he's quite a hunk, isn't he? This is big news in this village. People here would have been devastated if anything had happened to him. You're a local hero.'

Keira had a momentary vision of those compelling dark eyes. Even lying in the dust at her feet, Daniel Grant somehow managed to retain charisma. Yes, she could see why people thought such a lot of their GP.

With difficulty she shook herself free of the disturbing thoughts and turned back to the reporter. After all, the poor girl was only doing her job. 'OK, I'll do it, but please, don't make it sound like something out of a hospital drama. It was just a simple case of first aid, really it is.'

She posed obediently for a photo, and gave terse answers to questions, refusing to be drawn on her private life, and trying to keep the whole thing as low-key as possible.

'And what brought you to Penderby, Keira? Do you have friends in the village?'

'No, actually I — ' Then the church clock chimed the hour, cutting Keira off in mid sentence. She glanced up at it in horror. 'Oh, no!'

'What?'

'I was supposed to be at a job interview. Half an hour ago.'

'Where? You can have a lift if you like.' The policeman, now that he'd got over his shock, was anxious to be helpful.

'Just at the local veterinary practice. Acresfield Medical Centre. The vet's called Jim Bishop.'

'And he's right here.' A tall, well-built man with a bushy black beard stepped forward and took Keira's hand, pressing it warmly. 'I've just heard what you've been up to, young lady, and may I congratulate you on your considerable presence of mind. Well done.'

'Oh, I — ' Keira could feel the colour rushing to her cheeks. 'So, you think it will be all right? That I treated him — '

Jim grinned. 'It will probably be a nine days' wonder in the village, but of course it's all right. It's allowed for a vet to treat a human patient in an emergency. But if a doctor tries to treat an injured animal, then that's a different story. We don't let them trespass on our territory.'

'Yes, but — '

'But nothing. What else could you do? Sit there and let the man die?'

Keira looked away. Five years ago she remembered Miriam saying that death wasn't good enough for Daniel Grant. What would she have done in the circumstances?

'To be honest, I didn't have time to think about anything, I just had to get on with it. It's only now it's all over I worry that I did the right thing.'

'Think about it. If it had been the horse with the pneumothorax, rather than Daniel, what would you have done?'

'The same, I guess.'

'Well then.'

Keira exhaled slowly. 'OK, you win. I suppose one species is much like another. But how's the horse by the way?'

'I've checked her over and there's no damage done. Apparently she bolted when some motorbike backfired. Could have been a lot worse. A valuable animal that — temperamental though. You'll find that out when you get to know her better, she belongs to one of

19

our clients. Now come along with me, the least I can do is offer you a cup of tea.'

'Sorry?' Keira felt herself in danger of being swept away by a determined personality. Jim Bishop had already started to move off, and she put out a hand to stop him. 'Are you saying we should go and do the interview right now?'

He turned to her. 'Forget the interview, the job's yours if you want it. I already know that your qualifications are first rate, you've the right sort of experience, and after the way you acted under pressure just now I'd be proud to have you as one of the team.' He hesitated a moment, staring down into her face. 'That is, if you're interested? I don't want to rush you, especially on top of a stressful experience like you've just had. Maybe you'd prefer to look around the place first? After a bite of lunch?'

Keira looked away, her mind in a whirl. It was difficult to think straight.

She'd set out that morning with the full intention of accepting the job if it were offered to her, but now things were different. To be honest, she still felt shell-shocked. And she already knew that Acresfield Medical Centre housed the veterinary practice, a dentist and the local GPs' surgery, which meant that Daniel Grant — once he recovered — would be working right next door. She'd be bound to see a lot of him — something she hadn't exactly bargained for.

But at least she could look round the practice and give herself time to think. She managed a smile for Jim Bishop. 'Lunch sounds great. And then I'd love that guided tour.'

2

Keira was impressed. Both by the lunch, which was excellent, cooked by Jim's wife and part-time fellow-vet, Christine, who also acted as practice manager, and by the practice itself. Acresfield Medical Centre was built around converted steadings on the edge of Penderby village, but although externally it was all local stone and traditional farm architecture, inside it was the last word in up-to-date equipment.

'You've really invested a lot in the practice,' Keira commented as they finished their tour of the small animal hospital. A couple of post-op patients, a ginger cat and a dozy Jack Russell with one leg in plaster, surveyed her with interest through the bars of their cages.

'Yep, and hopefully it will pay dividends. We're particularly pleased with our diagnostic equipment. We share the automatic developers for our X-ray machine with the dental folk and the GPs — we can process the films right here on site in under five minutes.'

'How much contact do you have with the GPs?' Keira ventured, fingers crossed that Jim would respond 'very little' or words to that effect. But she was disappointed.

'Their surgery's the other side of the courtyard there; has its own separate entrance. But we share a dispensary, laundry and other facilities, like a coffee room for the staff, for example, and socially we all see quite a lot of each other which can't be bad.'

'Mmm.' Keira was non-committal.

Jim Bishop misinterpreted her. 'Looking forward to seeing more of Daniel?' He grinned. 'I hear you and he go back a long way.'

Keira blinked. How on earth did he know that? Was it really so obvious that she couldn't put Daniel Grant out of her mind? Or maybe the policeman had been passing on what she'd said. 'We knew each other slightly at university,' she said dismissively. 'He was a final year medic when I was first year in vet school. He was — a friend of a friend.'

'Ah. Well, I'm sure you'll have fun catching up on old times. I reckon he owes you dinner at the very least after what you did for him. People won't let him forget in a hurry.'

Keira digested this idea in silence. Perhaps she was being supersensitive, or was there just a hint of matchmaking in Jim's comments? If so, he was in for a profound disappointment. She deliberately changed the subject.

'You mentioned you'd got a new ultra-sound scanner? Could I have a look?'

'Sure. It's right here.'

Jim pushed open a door and ushered Keira into a small neat room. A heavily-pregnant Alsatian bitch, lying on a table, raised her head as they went over. A nurse was running the scanner over her abdomen, watched by the animal's anxious owner.

'Hi, Joyce, how's it going? Morning, Mrs Forbes.' Jim stared at the screen. 'What's the head count so far?'

'Five, and still rising. See for yourself.'

Keira watched as the screen revealed two more little bodies. The Alsatian thumped her tail.

'We'll have to keep a close eye on her,' Jim commented. 'That chap there looks as if he could be quite a size, what do you think, Keira?'

Before Keira could say anything, the dog owner interrupted. 'Keira, did you say? Keira Forrest? You must be the lady vet who operated on Dr Grant in the market square just now. How fantastic! Everybody's talking about it!'

Oh, not again! Keira had to restrain herself from rushing out of the room. The poor Alsatian was momentarily forgotten as she became the centre of attention. She mumbled a few responses to the eager questioning, and was very happy when she and Jim at last made their escape.

'I don't know if I can stand this.' She pushed her heavy fringe back from her forehead. 'I can't help feeling if this goes on I'll be a liability rather than an asset to the practice. You'd have people coming in just to ask me about open heart surgery in the town centre.'

'As long as they get charged for the privilege, who cares?' Jim laughed. Then, seeing that Keira wasn't smiling, he lowered his voice. 'Don't worry, they'll soon forget. This is a sleepy little place, there's not usually much drama here — so no wonder everyone's discussing you. Don't let that put you off taking the job, if you want it. As I said before, we'd be glad to have you working with us.'

Keira turned away and looked out of the window. Behind the steadings she could see the farmhouse where Jim and Christine lived, solid and comfortable with its grey stone walls and mossy slate roof. Above the old stable block gleamed the dormer windows of the little flat that went with the job. Beyond that, in a paddock, two ponies grazed. The job was everything she'd ever wanted — but that was before she'd bumped into Daniel Grant.

The thought of working almost literally alongside a man she despised was hard to take. Maybe she should look elsewhere. But then another thought truculently elbowed its way into her mind. Why should the presence of Daniel Grant put her off doing what she wanted to do? Why should something that was over and done with years ago still dictate the course of her life?

She turned back to Jim, suddenly decisive. 'Thanks.' She smiled up at him. 'I'd love to accept.'

'Brilliant! Come and have a drink to celebrate. Christine will be delighted. And you must meet our other colleague, Greg, he'll be back from his farm visits any time now.'

They set off back to the house, but as they approached, Christine came out to meet them. 'Jim, Greg phoned. There's a difficult calving up at the Kelman's farm — can you get up there'

'Sure, if you can hold the fort here. Sorry about this, Keira.'

'No problem. Actually, I'd better be getting back soon. I don't want to be in the way.'

'You're not in the way,' Christine assured her. 'In fact, I was hoping you could stay on longer because I just heard from the hospital that Daniel is doing well. Broken ribs, slight concussion, but his chest injury is stabilised, thanks to your prompt action, and there's no cranial damage. They said we could pop in to see him tonight. I thought you might like to come along, as it's on your way home. I'm sure he'd like to see you and thank you properly.'

Alarm bells sounded in Keira's mind. This was not at all what she'd had in mind; she intended giving Daniel Grant a wide berth, not standing vigil at his bedside. She started to frame an excuse. 'Surely he'll be tired, he'll only want to see close friends — '

'But you're an old friend of his, aren't you? Jim told me you knew each other at university.'

Keira sighed. No point in getting on the wrong side of her new employers, and she couldn't summon up the effort to explain things. She'd just drop by, say hello, and leave them to it. She could handle that. 'All right,' she conceded. 'But I can't stay long.'

'Brilliant. Now, I'm off on afternoon surgery — do you want to come and observe? It'll give you an idea of how we work here.'

The first customer was a honey-coloured guinea pig called Hazel, in to have her front teeth clipped. Her owner, a small boy of about ten glanced curiously at Keira.

'This is Miss Forest, Mark,' Christine explained. 'She's going to be working with us.'

The boy stared with growing interest. 'Is she the one who just saved Dr Grant's life?'

Christine grinned across at Keira as

she answered him. 'So you've heard about it, too. Yes, she is.'

'Would she do Hazel's teeth then? I'd like her to.'

Keira nodded, trying to hide her embarrassment behind a mask of professionalism. 'Sure. Will you hold her for me, Christine?'

She picked up the stainless steel clippers and examined the guinea pig's teeth. They certainly were long; the top ones had started to cut into the animal's bottom lip.

'You'll have to make sure she has something hard to chew on in future,' she told Mark as she got a grip on the first long incisor. 'Their teeth don't ever stop growing, so they need something to wear them down.'

The boy looked apprehensively at the clippers. 'Won't it hurt her?'

'No, there's no nerves this far down. This will just snap off — watch.'

She squeezed and the end of the tooth flew off to land with a startling ping in a steel bowl.

'Wow!' Mark was impressed.

She was soon able to hand Hazel back to the boy.

'I'll tell my mates I met you,' he informed her. 'I wish I'd been there when you did that operation on Dr Grant.'

'It wasn't as spectacular as your guinea pig's teeth,' Keira assured him.

Once he'd left she leaned against the treatment table and sighed. 'Am I never going to be allowed to forget this?'

'People are bound to be curious.' Christine was wiping over the table with antiseptic solution.

Keira enjoyed her afternoon, even though it was fairly routine stuff. Happily only a couple of clients — the guinea pig owner and a girl with an overweight cat — made any comment about Daniel Grant.

All too soon the surgery was over and she was following the Bishops into the local hospital. She was edgy, apprehensive. That reporter had been busy. Already there'd been two calls from

31

national newspapers, and the offer of an interview on local radio, which she had politely declined. Now, walking along the hospital corridor, she was wondering what memories Daniel would have of her? Of Miriam? He would have had time to think things over by now; would he feel shame for the way he'd acted? Or would he have put the whole episode neatly to one side? Five years was a long time. Maybe he'd be feeling too ill to think of it at all.

She lagged behind Jim and Christine as they went into the ward, unsure of what sort of greeting she'd get.

'There he is!' Jim pointed. 'And he's got a fan-club already. Typical!'

Daniel was lying in state in the end bed, a couple of vases of flowers already on his locker, and two student nurses chatting animatedly to him. A drip ran into his arm, his face was bruised down one side, and a cage protected his injured chest, but Keira could see that he was looking much better. Very much better.

She was unprepared for the surge of emotion that shot through her at the sight of him. Relief was uppermost, relief that her efforts on his behalf had been successful, and then genuine pleasure to see him looking so well. But, she reminded herself hastily, she'd feel the same way about any successful case. Hazel, the guinea pig, for example.

She waited, letting the Bishops go first, but soon they turned and beckoned her forward.

'Come on, Keira, why are you lurking back there?' Jim called out. 'It's you Daniel wants to see. This is the girl who saved your life,' he announced to the two nurses. 'Our new colleague.'

Keira, feeling very uncomfortable at being the centre of attention, walked forward and stood by the bed. She ran her tongue over her dry lips and summoned up an air of confidence she didn't feel. 'Hi, Daniel, how are you doing?'

He smiled up at her, and it was that

old, lazy smile that crinkled up the little lines at the corners of his eyes. She remembered it so well, though the creases had deepened a little with the years, and those dark eyes were shadow smudged.

'I'm fine, thanks to you.' His voice was quiet, but it resonated through her. She could feel her pulse rate accelerating. 'I don't know how I can ever thank you.'

'Oh, please, enough of the drama. I'm not cut out to be a heroine. I just did what needed doing.'

'Not exactly your field though, is it? What did you do — imagine you were dealing with a sick animal?'

Despite herself, Keira laughed. 'Something like that. One mammal is very like another really.' She warmed to the theme. 'Actually, the last time I performed that procedure, it was on a sheep with bloat.'

Jim's shout of laughter had half the ward staring in their direction. 'I hope you gave that quote to the newspapers!

Seriously, Dan, you and this lass are going to be front page news in the local rag tomorrow. I wouldn't be surprised if it makes it to the national dailies.

'How do you feel about that, Keira?' Daniel was watching her intently. 'You never were one for the limelight, were you?'

Keira felt a jolt of surprise. She'd never realised Daniel had particularly noticed her, and his perceptiveness was startling. 'No, I wasn't,' she said lamely. 'I hope it will all have died down by the time I start work here.'

'When's that to be?'

'Next month.'

'Great.' He smiled up at her again. 'I'll be back on my feet by then; we've got a lot of catching up to do.' He stopped for a moment. 'How's Steve, by the way?'

Keira bit her lip, summoning up a detached tone of voice. That wound was nearly healed now, but not so completely that a chance remark like this couldn't reopen it.

'Steve's not in the picture any more,' she managed. 'We split up at the end of last year.'

'Oh. I'm sorry to hear that.'

Did he really mean it? It didn't really matter. Daniel Grant's opinions were neither here nor there, she reminded herself. But across the bed Keira could see Jim and Christine beaming like indulgent parents; behind them the two nurses were looking on in frank jealousy. She felt trapped, there was nothing she could do to get out of this without looking foolish.

Then, she remembered. 'By the way — ' She looked very directly into Daniel's eyes, wanting to see his reaction to what she was going to say. 'You haven't asked after Miriam.'

There! She'd got him. She saw that by the flicker of emotion he couldn't quite manage to hide. He was silent for a couple of seconds, then he said, 'Ah — Miriam. So the two of you are still in touch. How is she?'

'She's fine — now. She dropped out of medical school; she has a secretarial job with an oil company.'

The easy atmosphere was wrecked. Keira heard Jim Bishop clear his throat, obviously sensing that something wasn't quite right. She felt uncomfortable at deliberately opening these old wounds, but she had to be loyal to Miriam. After the way this guy had behaved, he deserved to be reminded of it from time to time.

'Sorry, I must be on my way,' she managed, dredging up a smile from somewhere. 'I'll leave you in peace.'

Without waiting for a reply she turned on her heel and walked out of the ward. Her mind was a chaos of conflicting emotions.

She'd agreed to take on the new job, but what else was she taking on? How was she going to be able to cope with the situation she found herself in?

And what about Miriam? If — when — all this got into the national newspapers she'd be bound to read about it, or if not, some well-meaning person would inevitably tell her. I'd better make sure I phone her tonight and get to her first with the news.

3

'Keira, the man ruined my life! Don't you understand?' Even over the phone Miriam's anguish was plain. Five years had apparently made no difference to her resentment towards Daniel Grant.

Keira put up a hand and eased the heavy fall of hair from the nape of her neck. She sighed to herself; Miriam was reacting just like she'd been afraid she would. She was deeply attached to her friend — they'd been through a lot together — but if only she could persuade Miriam not to dwell so much on the past —

She tried again. 'Look, I know he behaved badly, and I'm not trying to make any excuses for him, but — '

'Badly? He practically left me at the altar! He was a complete rat! We had everything planned, Keira. We'd — '

'I know all that, love.' Keira kept her tone gentle. 'But, well, it is over five years ago now. Isn't it time you put it all behind you?'

'I thought I had!' Miriam wailed. 'But all this has brought it back to me. I can't tell you what it was like, reading about you and him in the paper this morning. Why couldn't you have told me about it yourself?'

'I tried to. I phoned last night, but you were out, and it wasn't the sort of news I wanted to leave on the answering machine. And anyway, in the end I took the phone off the hook, there were so many reporters calling.'

'Didn't you remember he came from that part of the country? He often used to talk about it,' Miriam asked.

'Not to me.' She took a deep breath. 'Anyway, look, I have to tell you, I've agreed to take the job, apart from having Daniel Grant in the surgery next door, it's exactly what I wanted.'

'Well, don't expect me to come visiting! And I shouldn't think any of our other friends will want to come either.'

'Oh, Miriam!' Keira was on the verge of losing patience. 'I don't want us to fall out over this.'

'I'm not the one falling out. I'm not the one stirring up old memories.'

'And neither am I, not on purpose. I hope you will come and see me — I can find out when Daniel's away, if you like. Then you'd be sure of not bumping into him. This is a wonderful place, really peaceful, you'd love it.'

'Well, maybe. But I wouldn't trust myself to keep my temper if I met him again. I'd tell him exactly what I thought of him. Remember, Keira, after he left me I was so frantic I took that overdose. I could have died. He must have known about it, but did he bother to get in touch? No!'

Keira was silent for a few moments, remembering. Yes, it had been a terrible two weeks, even five years on, it still made her shudder.

Perhaps she was being unsympathetic, and unrealistic in expecting

Miriam to get over Daniel quite so easily. But she had to keep trying. 'Look, Miriam, don't dwell on all that,' she urged. 'It was ghastly at the time, and I'm really sorry that I've dredged it all up again for you, but you've got to look forward not back. You've got a new life now, think of all the good things, not the bad.'

There was silence for a couple of seconds, then Miriam heaved a sigh. 'You're right, Keira. I'll try to be positive — it was just a shock that's all. But will you do one thing for me?'

'Of course I will. What is it?'

'You — you won't get involved with Daniel yourself, will you? I know how it is in these little villages, and he's an attractive man. I couldn't stand it if that happened.'

'Oh, come on!' Keira tried to hang on to her patience. 'Just because I performed a bit of minor surgery doesn't mean we're a couple. No, there is no way I'm going to get involved with Daniel.'

'Promise?'

'Promise.'

Keira felt on safe ground. After all, Daniel hadn't been attracted to her back at university, so why should he be now? She wasn't his type — not conventionally pretty, not bubbly and outgoing like her friend had been.

Deliberately she changed the subject, saddened that Miriam still harboured such bitter memories. When she eventually put the phone down she felt emotionally drained. If she'd known how it was going to complicate things, maybe she'd never have applied for that job. But she had, and she'd got it, and she had to get on with life. It was as simple as that. At least, she hoped so.

Four weeks later Jim and Christine Bishop threw a party in their home to welcome Keira to Acresfield Medical Centre. There were two dozen or so people in the comfortable sitting-room, drinking wine and nibbling sandwiches, all in her honour — 'Come and meet our new colleague,' Jim had invited

43

— but there was no sign of Daniel Grant. Keira didn't know how to take it. Relief or disappointment, which?

'I'm Greg McKenzie, the other vet in the practice.' A tallish stocky man with sandy hair and a pronounced Scots accent, advanced on her and kissed her cheek. Keira murmured something in response, trying to channel her attention back to the people who were there, rather than the one who wasn't.

'I do most of the large animal work,' Greg was saying. 'I expect you'd want to concentrate on the smaller stuff.'

He had her attention now and no mistake. 'I don't know about that! I quite enjoyed the large animal work at college, and I hoped that in a country practice like this there'd be plenty of opportunity for me to get out to the farms — at least that's what Jim led me to believe. I don't mind getting my hands dirty, I can assure you.'

Greg held up his hands in mock surrender. 'Sorry, sorry! Guess I touched a raw nerve there.'

Keira had to smile. 'Fraid you did. Sorry if I overreacted.'

'No problem. Can I get you a drink?'

'Thanks. A white wine and soda would be nice.'

Greg went off to get her drink and Keira found her attention claimed by a couple of young veterinary nurses. 'I can't understand what's happened to Dr Grant,' one of them was saying.

'So he was expected, then?' Keira asked.

'Sure. You'll want to meet him, I bet, to see the results of your bit of first aid.'

Keira smiled non-commitally. 'Well, it's always nice to see how a patient's getting on. Mine can't usually tell me how they feel, though.'

'Well, now's your chance to find out,' one of the girls squealed excitedly. 'Here he is.'

Keira wasn't ready for the surge of adrenaline that shot through her. Her mouth was suddenly dry as she accepted the glass of wine that Greg had brought. Daniel was talking to Jim and Christine, but his eyes were searching the room, and Keira knew he was looking for her.

He saw her, and waved, saying something to Jim and Christine. A moment later he was right in front of her, his smile hers alone.

'Hello, Keira, good to see you. Sorry I'm late, we had a suspected gall bladder case, but in the end it turned out to be simple over-indulgence.' He drew her to him, and his lips grazed her cheek. 'Welcome to Acresfield.'

Keira felt herself tensing. She'd known this would probably happen, and tried to prepare for it, but the brief formal kiss aroused echoes all through her body. Like it or not, the old attraction was still there and it flared at his touch. Somehow she clung on to her composure, hoping desperately that he wouldn't notice her reaction, and with an effort she managed to keep her tone casual. 'So you're back to normal, then?'

'Pretty well, though the ribs aren't

quite there yet. But as far as I'm concerned I'm fine — and for that I'm in your debt. I owe you more than I can say.'

He was staring down at her with an intensity that brought the heat to her skin. Oh no, she thought despairingly. He must feel under some sort of obligation; I saved his life and now he thinks he's expected to do something to repay me.

The idea of Daniel Grant regarding her as his personal guardian angel was not a welcome one. It didn't quite fit in with her determination to maintain a coolly polite professional, but distant, relationship.

'Look, we've got to get over this. What I did was pure first aid — OK, so it saved your life, but so? You're a GP, you must be used to saving people's lives. All in a day's work for you.'

Daniel smiled. 'I wouldn't say that. In a small place like Penderby most of what I have to deal with is sniffles, indigestion, ante-natal patients, that sort of thing. Hardly ER type stuff. But, yes, we do get some life-threatening cases.'

'Right. And you don't expect them to be forever trying to thank you for your help.' She knew she was gabbling, but somehow she couldn't stop. 'I mean, the other day I had to treat this cat called Charlie, he was run over by a car and you wouldn't have given tuppence for him when they brought him in, poor chap. Anyway, to cut a long story short, I was able to operate and he came through. Now, Charlie's owner isn't going to thank me ceaselessly for saving his cat's life, is he?'

'I take your point.' Daniel's grin had broadened. 'OK, I won't embarrass you any more. But, do you know, that's the longest little speech you've ever made to me? I used to think you were a person of very few words.'

Keira forced a smile. 'Well, I was just trying to get things straight. I don't usually rabbit on like this.'

'No problem. Let's change the

subject. We've a lot to catch up on. What have you been doing over the last five years?'

'For a start, getting qualified.' She felt relieved, back on safe ground. She'd rehearsed this particular little speech, knowing that she'd have to make it at some point. It tripped off her tongue easily enough — dates, places, people. Nothing at all about her private life — she might as well have been talking to a complete stranger.

'How about yourself?' she asked at last, feeling that it was the polite thing to do. She was surprised by the reply she got.

'I'm not long back in Britain, actually; I've only been in this job about six months. Before that I was working in Africa, Zambia, in fact, helping set up a hospital.'

'Really? That can't have been easy.'

'Easy, no, but very rewarding. Life is a constant round of making do. No disposable equipment as we have here; everything is sterilised and re-used, just as it used to be. And there are flies everywhere, you just can't get rid of them, even in the operating theatre.'

Keira shuddered. 'It makes you think, doesn't it? When here, even household pets usually have their operations carried out in a sterile environment.'

'Right. And the people are glad of whatever they can get, out there in the bush. It was quite common for people to queue for a clinic for twenty-four hours at a time, having walked miles to get there. The spirit is incredible, a real inspiration.'

'I can see that.' Keira was fascinated. 'But what made you go — '

'Hi, Daniel, got a drink?' Jim Bishop bumbled up behind them, beer in hand. 'Can't have you monopolising Keira like this, there are lots of people wanting to meet her. Come on, Keira, I want to introduce you to our friends in the dental practice.'

There was no arguing with Jim. Keira was borne off to meet the dentist, a young blond man with the build of a prop forward, while Daniel was claimed by the two veterinary nurses. Keira managed to make polite conversation, but her mind was far away in Zambia. Had Daniel gone out there because of a selfless desire to help underprivileged people? Or deliberately to run away from his responsibilities?

The next day Keira smoothed down her green overall and took a last look around the consulting room. Everything seemed to be in order. She smiled at the young veterinary nurse. 'OK, Lianne, let's have the first one through, shall we?' She felt a thrill of anticipation. Her first proper patient here at Acresfield. And hopefully, by now people would have forgotten about that bit of minor surgery on Dr Grant. She was ready with a casually dismissive remark just in case they hadn't.

She heard the patient before she saw it. A frenzied shrieking was coming from a wire basket, carried in by a very worried-looking elderly woman. Lianne helped her lift the basket on to the table and Keira looked at the spitting bundle of fury inside.

'He's not a happy chap. What seems to be the problem?'

'He's hurt his paw,' the woman explained. 'It's been swollen for a day or two; I thought he'd got a grass seed or something in it, but he won't let me near enough to see, will you, petal?'

She leaned forward and put a finger through the bars, only to have it nearly taken off by a swipe from the cat's good paw.

'Oh dear, we'd better have a look,' Keira said with as much confidence as she could muster.

She opened the door of the box, prepared for a rush, but the black and white cat retreated to the back, snarling a warning.

'Give me a hand, Lianne. We'll have to tip him out. Can you stand back, Mrs er — '

'Mrs Grainger. He's not like this usually, you know. I have six cats, and they're all such good-natured animals. His name's Fred, by the way.'

'OK.' Keira, deciding that discretion was the better part of valour, put on a pair of heavy gauntlets. 'Right, Lianne.'

The nurse upended the container, gently tipping the bewildered cat on to the treatment table. Before he could react, Keira seized him firmly, pinioning his front legs. Lianne came forward with a thick blanket, which together they wrapped round him, leaving just his head free, spitting curses.

'Which paw was it?'

'Er — front right, I think. No, left. Oops, sorry.'

Keira, unwrapping the cat's good right paw had narrowly escaped having her sleeve shredded by his outstretched claws. With an effort she rewrapped him, and managed, after a slight struggle, to free the injured limb. 'Oh my, I can see why he's in such a bad mood, poor creature. Look, Lianne, he's got an ingrown claw. It's digging into his paw, probably causing an infection.'

'Oh dear.' Mrs Grainger came over to see. 'Poor Fred.'

'It's just like having an in-growing toenail, just as painful.' Keira examined the offending claw, ignoring Fred's curses. 'But it shouldn't take a second to get it out. I'll warn you, he won't like it though.'

Lianne passed over a pair of small cutters, and Keira quickly severed the claw and pulled out the end that was stuck into the paw. As she cleaned up the small wound Fred hissed savagely and struggled for freedom in vain.

'That's it out. Look, he's calming down already.' Keira smiled. 'I'll give him an injection of antibiotic, and you can have a course of tablets to take home for him. The swelling should settle in a day or two, but if it doesn't, bring him back.'

She hoped devoutly that she wouldn't be seeing Fred again, unless he was in a better mood. Lianne opened the box and he slunk back in, quite clearly pleased to have some privacy.

'Oh, thank you.' Mrs Grainger was all smiles. 'I'm so pleased you sorted him out so quickly. 'Would you mind if I left him here in his carrier for a few minutes? I've got an appointment myself over the way with Doctor Grant. Such a wonderful doctor, he is. Very understanding. Oh, but I was forgetting; you know him very well, don't you, Miss Forrest?'

Keira returned her smile. 'I'm sure you'll be in good hands,' she said, wanting to change the subject before it moved on to operations in the market square. 'Hope it's not as traumatic for you as it was for Fred.'

'No, the doctor's trying to persuade me to get my hip done. He keeps on about it, but he's wasting his breath. I can manage perfectly well as I am.'

She walked towards the door and Keira noticed that she did have a pronounced limp. It looked as though Dr Grant had a point.

Thankfully the next few patients were all more amenable than Fred. As the last one, an elderly retriever in for a booster, ambled out, Keira leaned against the table. 'I don't know about you, Lianne, but I'm ready for my lunch. I — '

'Keira, hold everything.' The consulting room door flew open, and Sally, the receptionist, put her head round. 'An RTA, Doctor Grant's just bringing it in.'

'Dr Grant?' Keira said.

'Yeah, he was giving old Mrs Grainger a lift home from the surgery and he saw the dog by the side of the road. He'd dropped Mrs G off, thank heaven, anyway, he phoned us straight away. He'll be here any minute — in fact, here he is.'

'Where shall I put him?' Daniel was in the room, carrying a blood-stained shaggy bundle that lay limp in his arms.

'Here, on the table.' Keira caught her breath; the dog, who looked in a dreadful state, claimed a hundred per cent of her attention. 'Can you bring the oxygen over, Lianne? And we'll need to set up a drip. Daniel, are you OK to hold him, in case he struggles? Mind you, he doesn't look in a fit state to start anything, he seems pretty dazed. Was it your car that hit him?'

'No, although it nearly did.' Daniel carefully placed the unresisting dog on the treatment table, while Lianne came over with the oxygen mask and the clippers. 'He — if it is a he — was collapsed just on the verge. Some other car must have caught him and not stopped, can you believe it?'

Keira was giving the dog a general checkover, running her hands over the animal's outstretched limbs. 'Just put the mask near his face, Lianne, I don't want to upset him by fixing it on. I'll deal with the drip.'

After a couple of minutes' examination and a check that the drip was functioning she straightened up. 'Well, it's not as bad as I thought. The only damage I can see immediately is this bang on the head — that's where the car must have hit him. He might have a skull fracture, and that could be serious, but it's the scalp damage that's caused all the bleeding. I'll have to stitch it. I can't find any other injuries, but he's got a bad case of mange to add to his other problems.'

She glanced up from the passive dog at Daniel's bloodstained shirt and trousers. 'Perhaps you should get away home and clean yourself up; looking like that you might give your patients a shock.'

Daniel looked down at himself. 'How right you are. Lord, what a mess. I'll come over first thing in the morning to see how he is. Good luck.'

He went out, and as the door closed behind him Keira was surprised to find that she'd hardly given him a thought. All her attention had been focussed on the animal who needed her help. This had to be progress.

4

True to his word, Daniel appeared in the surgery first thing the next morning. Keira was prepared for him, she managed to pull off a detached but friendly smile and concentrated her thoughts on the injured dog. 'He's recovered surprisingly quickly. And the good news is that the X-ray showed only a hairline fracture of the skull. Nothing else — no sign of inter-cranial damage. I've stitched up the scalp wound and given him a shot of antibiotic. I took a skin scraping while I was at it, and like I thought, he has dermodectic mange. He'll need regular baths in an antibiotic solution to clear it. Other than that, it's looking good.

'That's good news.' Daniel's relief was evident. 'Can I have a look at him?'

'Sure.' Keira hesitated only slightly. She hadn't bargained for Daniel taking such an interest in the dog, but as long as his interest was focussed solely on the animal she was confident that she could cope.

As they approached he raised his head and gently thumped his tail in welcome.

'Friendly chap, isn't he, despite everything.' Daniel commented. 'I wonder who his owners are; they'll be frantic.'

Keira frowned. 'I'm not too hopeful about finding them, actually. In fact, all the signs are that he's been abandoned.'

'What? What makes you say that?'

'Well, his claws are quite worn down, and his pads too. That's consistent with him running a long way on a tarmac surface.'

Daniel swore under his breath. 'You mean some callous so-and-so tipped him out of the car and then drove off, knowing he was running along behind trying to catch up?'

'I'm afraid so. Ghastly, isn't it? But it happens a lot, I'm sad to say.'

Daniel crouched down and put out a hand to the dog, who licked it. When he spoke his voice was gruff. 'Why would they do a thing like that?

'Probably because they couldn't cope with him. You see, this chap is just a puppy; he's got a lot of growing to do yet. I'd say he's an Irish wolfhound, or perhaps a deerhound — difficult to tell at the moment because he's so undernourished. He'll get to be quite a size before he's finished, and perhaps his owners felt they simply didn't have space for him.'

'So why not take him to the RSPCA?' Daniel demanded.

Keira shrugged. 'Who knows. That's where we'll take him, once he's fit enough, if no-one claims him. Poor chap, he deserves a chance.'

Gently Daniel patted the puppy's shoulder before he stood up. 'Well, he's going to get one. I'll have him if no-one claims him.'

'You?' She stared at him. This evidence of compassion on the part of

Daniel Grant was a new concept, and one that she had to struggle with. For the past few years she'd thought of him — when she thought of him at all — as callousness personified. Then she felt guilty for thinking badly of him. People could change.

'He'll need plenty of exercise; how will you manage that?'

Daniel thought for a moment, then he said, 'He'll come out with me on my morning run, and I can take him out again at night. The neighbours will let him out at lunchtime if I'm not home — you're welcome to take him yourself if you like. My house is just down the lane.'

Keira was tempted; she'd always loved big dogs, and had a soft spot for the gentle-natured wolfhounds. Their ferocious appearance belied their affectionate disposition. But she forced herself to think how Miriam or any of her other friends would react if they learned that she was walking Daniel Grant's dog. This was only her second day in the job, for heaven's sake, and already she was in danger of getting in deep.

She took a step away, and forced a dismissive tone into her voice. 'You seem to have it all covered. So if no-one claims him he's yours. If you need any help one of the nurses can give you leaflets and advice about diet or training.'

She turned away, not wanting to look at him, that was his cue to go away, but he didn't seem to realise. He was still standing there, she knew.

Suddenly there was a burst of electronic music; after a moment's startled incomprehension Keira recognised it as the ring tone of a mobile. She swung round to find Daniel reaching into his pocket.

'Sorry, I'm on a call. I'll just take this outside.'

He went out, reappearing a couple of minutes later. 'Bad news, I'm afraid. An elderly patient has had a fall. She's a woman with a lot of cats — '

'Not Mrs Grainger?'

'That's her. You must have met one of the cats already — can't say I'm surprised. Anyway, it seems she's tripped over one of them. I must go and see how she is. And it's lucky you're here, she's asking for a vet as well. Are you free to come along? Apparently she's worried about the cat.'

Keira was relieved to be on safe, professional ground; she was determined to keep it that way.

Ten minutes later they were at Mrs Grainger's cottage. A young, harassed-looking woman let them in. 'Mum's got her foot up on the sofa,' she explained. 'She says it's all right, but I don't think so.' She looked curiously at Keira then recognition dawned. 'Aren't you the lady vet who — '

'That's right,' Daniel said quickly. 'But today her patient is the cat.' He winked at Keira. 'I'm the one who'll be treating your mother, I hope she won't be too disappointed.'

Keira followed him inside, amused at

the deft way he forestalled any questions about the marketplace incident. Maybe he was as fed up of it as she was.

They found a pale-faced Mrs Grainger sitting on the sofa, cradling a large tabby cat. 'Oh, Doctor, I'm so sorry to bother you! It would have waited, but Jennifer insisted on phoning. And Miss Forrest too!' She gave Daniel a sly glance of approval as she knelt down to look at her swollen ankle. 'Good to see the two of you getting on so well — ouch!'

'A bit tender there?' Daniel looked up. 'Suppose you let Keira take the cat off you — is he the one responsible?'

'He is, poor dear.' Mrs Grainger passed the animal over to Keira. 'His name's Arthur. I do hope he's all right.'

Arthur turned out to be a much more docile proposition than Fred had been. Keira examined him carefully and could find no sign of injury. 'Cats are good at getting out of the way,' she commented. 'There's one thing that worries me though, he seems to have a persistent dry cough. There he goes again. How long has he had it?'

'Oh, he's always like that,' Mrs Grainger said. 'Doesn't seem to do him any harm. I've got used to it.'

'Maybe you should bring him in to the surgery some time then. We might be able to do something for him. How's Fred, by the way?'

'He's fine. He ran outside when he heard you coming though, I'm afraid you're not his favourite person.'

Keira refrained from commenting that Fred was not exactly her favourite cat — poor beast, he probably had a gentle unassuming personality under different circumstances. She knew that vets often saw the worst side of their patients — maybe doctors did too. 'How's the ankle doing?' she asked.

Daniel finished his examination and stood up. 'I'd say it was just a sprain, but to be on the safe side I'd like to get it X-rayed. Tomorrow morning will do, but you must keep off it in the meantime. I'll strap it up for you just now — have you any elastic bandage in the house?'

'I reckon we have. I never throw anything away.' Mrs Grainger gave instructions to her daughter, then turned back to Daniel and Keira. 'Can I offer you a cup of tea or anything?'

Keira answered for both of them. 'I think we should let you have a rest, Mrs Grainger. You've had a shock.'

'Quite right,' Daniel approved, starting to bandage the foot. 'And I want to talk to you about that hip, Mrs G. If you weren't quite so unstable on your legs you might not have fallen. With a new hip you'd be good as new — we'd have you racing about like one of those moggies of yours.'

Mrs Grainger sighed. 'Well, maybe. This has made me think. I'll see how I feel about it tomorrow, Doctor.'

As they drove away, Daniel shook his head. 'By tomorrow morning she'll have had time to remember all the old excuses — too long away from her cats, hating the idea of being in hospital, suppose something goes wrong. I'll have my work cut out to persuade her. But how about that cat? You seemed concerned about it.'

'I was. It could be a chest infection. I'd like to check it over.'

'Well, I guarantee that Mrs G. will be more concerned about that than about her hip. I wish I could get her to take more care of herself.'

'Then why don't you stress the cat angle?' Keira suggested. 'Point out what would happen if she was immobile and couldn't look after them.'

'Sounds like emotional blackmail to me.' Daniel slanted her a sideways glance. 'I didn't know you went in for that.'

There was a slight chill to his tone that didn't go unnoticed. 'I didn't mean it like that. But as long as you weren't too heavy about it, it might help.'

As they passed the old church the clock struck two. 'I don't know about you,' Daniel commented, 'but I think lunch is long overdue. We could stop off at my place and have an omelette or something if you like.'

An alarm bell shrilled in Keira's mind. 'That's very kind,' she said carefully, 'but I ought to be getting on with my unpacking, there's still lots of it to do. I'd better go straight back.'

They reached the Acresfield stable block, and Keira got out of the car. 'Thanks for the lift. I — I'll see you around.'

Without waiting for a reply she got out of the car and hurried into the surgery. Oh, what a way to act! She felt like a self-conscious teenager.'

But somehow the Daniel Grant Keira was meeting in Acresfield didn't fit into that mould at all. All right, she hadn't seen that much of him yet, but he seemed to be well liked and respected — held in affection, even. And his reaction to the injured dog had been pure compassion.

Could someone change as radically as all that she wondered, as she put away the equipment she'd taken to Mrs

Grainger's. Maybe Daniel had had a life-changing experience in Africa.

Her eyes opened wide at this new prospect, but then she shook her head with a wry smile. Unlikely.

5

Keira walked unhurriedly down to the village shop, still, after nearly a fortnight, amazed at her good luck in getting a job in this idyllic place. Ducks splashed in the pond across the green, fed by a group of young children and their mothers, while on the other side of the road, cottage gardens blazed in a kaleidoscope of colour — a scene that could hardly have changed much for generations.

She went into the small supermarket armed with a list of basic groceries to replenish her stocks. A few people greeted her; already she was getting known around the village. Thankfully the Daniel Grant incident had become old news; at least no-one mentioned it any more.

In the dairy section Mrs Grainger bore down on her, leaning heavily on her trolley, which was laden with tinned cat food.

'Morning, Miss Forrest.'

'Mrs Grainger, hello! How are the cats?'

A mistake. Keira found herself imprisoned against the cheese counter while Mrs Grainger discoursed at length about her cats, mainly Arthur, whose cough was still causing concern, despite the course of antibiotics Keira had prescribed.

'I've tried giving him glycerine to soothe his throat, but he's no better. Do you think it might be something infectious?'

'I'd really need to see him,' Keira said. 'There could be any number of causes; I'm beginning to wonder if he might be asthmatic. Perhaps you could phone in for an appointment.'

'I'll do that. And, oh, Miss Forrest, don't you buy that cheese here. You'll get it down on the market for half the price and much better quality. I know you vets earn a fortune, but there's no sense in throwing money away, is there?'

Keira had to smile, even though she felt that her salary as a newly-qualified vet would not quite match up to Mrs Grainger's high expectations. Also, the assistant at the cheese counter was staring at them with undisguised hostility after hearing the comments on her carefully-arranged produce. Perhaps it was time to leave.

'I'd love to have a look at the market,' she began, 'but there are a few things I need here. I'll — '

The next minute the quiet calm of the little supermarket was shattered. There was a sudden crash from near the door, followed by the sound of galloping feet. People ran for cover, trolleys collided, one overturned shedding its contents.

Someone shouted, 'It's that wretched dog of the doctor's!'

Round the corner of the aisle, scattering a display of baked beans, erupted a shaggy grey animal, barking furiously. He skidded on the tiled floor, legs flailing; by some miracle Mrs Grainger managed to side-step out of his way.

The manager came into view, frantically waving his arms from a safe distance. 'Catch him, somebody!'

No-one seemed willing to try, until Keira, after a few seconds' paralysed amazement, reached out as the hound set off again, and grabbed his collar. For a moment she thought she was about to be dragged up the aisle in his wake, but then, to her surprise he sat down, suddenly docile and licked her hand.

The manager hurried up to her. Keira recognised him as the owner of a sedate black poodle who had been brought in for inoculations the previous week. He glanced scornfully at the hound puppy.

'Miss Forrest, thank goodness you were here! That creature might have wrecked the place.'

Keira glanced round at the scattered

baked bean tins and the overturned display of greeting cards that had been the first casualty of the escaped dog's reckless progress. 'He had a pretty good try, didn't he? But in fairness, I think it was people shrieking at him that made him rush about and bump into things; he was probably only trying to find the way out. Now I suppose I'd better take him home.'

'That would be good of you — but, no need. His owner's put in an appearance.'

Daniel was coming up the aisle, looking suitably contrite. He approached the manager. 'Peter, what can I say? Finn, you bad boy! I don't know how on earth he got out, he must have jumped the fence.'

'Looks like you'd better get a higher one.' The manager was not impressed.

'Obedience classes, that's what he needs,' Mrs Grainger suddenly piped up. Other shoppers had gathered round and there were nods of agreement.

'You're quite right,' Daniel said

resignedly, 'and don't think I haven't enquired. But the nearest ones are ten miles away.'

'Get the vet to do it,' someone suggested. Everyone, including Daniel, looked at Keira.

She was at a loss. 'I don't know, I — '

'You'd be doing the village a service,' Mrs Grainger put in. 'And saving Dr Grant a lot of worry.'

Keira felt herself weakening. She had a soft spot for the dog — he'd made an excellent recovery but after his horrendous start in life he needed some help. And if Daniel couldn't keep control of him he might have to go for re-homing after all; he deserved a better chance than that.

Finn looked up at her, his brown eyes trusting and licked her hand again.

'OK,' she conceded. 'I'll have a go.'

There was a murmur of approval from the onlookers, while Daniel's relief was evident in his broad grin. 'Keira, you're a star! I'll be in touch to arrange a time.'

Keira took the opportunity to make her escape down the household goods aisle, loading a few random items into her trolley while she thought over what she'd just done. Obedience classes, for heaven's sake! For someone determined to avoid Daniel Grant as much as possible, she wasn't succeeding very well.

'What's this I hear about you?' Christine Bishop asked later that morning, as she sat at Keira's small kitchen table having a mug of coffee. Keira meanwhile was staring in disbelief at the items she'd apparently bought while her mind was on another planet.

'Why ever did I get this?' she asked, holding up a packet of firelighters. 'I don't even have a fire.'

'I'll have them,' Christine offered. 'They'll be handy for the barbeque. We're having one tomorrow for Sunday lunch, by the way, I hope you can come.'

'Thanks, I'd love to. I'd gone out to

buy myself something for tomorrow's lunch, but somehow I seem to have forgotten.'

'Well, it's worked out OK then, hasn't it? But I'm not surprised you bought the wrong things if what I heard is true. Were you actually set upon in the supermarket by Daniel Grant's dog?'

'Oh, honestly!' Keira leaned against the worktop and raised her eyes to heaven. 'Does absolutely everything get exaggerated in this village? No, I wasn't set upon, far from it, but,' she couldn't help laughing, 'you should have seen everyone scatter when Finn charged in! Even that fat farmer — you know, the one who wasn't keen on having me dehorn his cattle — anyway, he moved like greased lightning.'

'Serve him right for being such a chauvinist,' Christine commented dryly. 'Oh well, maybe it wasn't quite as dramatic as I was led to believe, but I did hear that you actually agreed to take the mutt on as an obedience pupil.

You're going to have your work cut out there.'

'He's not a mutt!' Keira sprang to Finn's defence. 'He has the makings of a very handsome Irish wolfhound, especially now that the mange has cleared up. I have every confidence that I can make something of him.'

'And Daniel?' Christine prompted, smiling. 'Can you make anything of him?'

'What do you mean?' Keira pasted on an answering smile but her heart wasn't in it.

'What do you think? Everyone can see that he's taking a very definite interest in you, and not just because of that bit of ER in the market place. He's forever popping in to the surgery.'

Keira made a dismissive gesture. 'So? He needs things for Finn. He was in on Monday for dog meal, and then he came to look at baskets. Oh, and he was asking about making a run for Finn so that he can't escape again, and then he wanted to buy a lead — '

'Hmm. And of course you've agreed to help train Finn — '

'Yes, but that's pure public spiritedness, honestly.'

'More than that, I'd say. I think you two must have been closer friends than you let on, back at university.'

For one crazy moment Keira was within a heartbeat of telling Christine everything. How Daniel had behaved to Miriam, how he'd brought her to the brink of suicide. That would stop the rumours in their tracks.

But she couldn't do it. Couldn't bring herself to wreck Daniel's good name. Whatever he'd done years ago, that was over now. These people knew nothing of it, she had no right to rake up the past.

She turned away under pretext of refilling her mug from the kettle. 'Sorry to disappoint you, but we weren't close at all. It was my friend he was interested in, not me, and then when that relationship fizzled out I didn't see anything more of him. And before you ask — ' she turned to Christine with what she hoped was a very sincere and convincing expression. 'I have no plans to change the situation. I'm not looking for romance, believe me.'

Christine sighed. 'Oh dear, what a disappointment. Looks like it leaves the way clear for Fiona Barstow then.'

'Who's she?'

'The owner of the riding school. She's had the hots for Daniel ever since he showed his face in the village, and I suppose yes, he has showed some interest in her. More than that, if some folk are to be believed. She's quite attractive, but personally I don't think she's his type.'

Keira sat down at the table. She'd been unprepared for the stab of jealousy — what else could it be? — when Christine had made her bland announcement. But why shouldn't Daniel have a girlfriend?

'Ironically enough,' Christine was saying, 'it was one of Fiona's horses that caused Daniel's accident. The chestnut mare. You might like to go up to the stables sometime and see her. Greg is our horse expert, but I'm sure he'd be pleased to take you up to the riding school and show you around.'

Keira took a deep breath, blanking out thoughts of Daniel and Fiona Barstow. She just about meant it when she said, 'Yes, I'd like that. Now that I've convinced Greg that I can be trusted with large animals he might actually let me do something with the horses.'

'And so he should. He did grudgingly admit to me that you were pretty capable with dehorning those cows the other day, and coming from Greg that's praise. If he didn't have a fiancée in Arbroath, I'd be tempted to do a bit of matchmaking there.'

She ducked as Keira threatened to hurl a wet dishcloth.

Sunday morning Keira awoke to cloudless blue skies. It looked like Jim and Christine would have a wonderful day for their barbeque. She got up and showered then ate a bowl of cereal, shaking her head at the sugar-coated frosty flakes. Hadn't she intended to buy muesli?

There was nothing needing doing in the little flat, so Keira decided to go and see if she could be any help with the barbeque preparations. She knew that Jim had been on call the previous evening, so it was possible that he might not have got much sleep.

Just as she was about to set out, the phone rang.

'Hello, Keira Forrest here.'

'Keira, it's me, Daniel.'

She made a grab for the phone that had slipped through her suddenly nerveless fingers. Daniel was the last person she'd expected. 'Hi,' she managed. 'What can I do for you?'

'Professional call. I'm at the riding school — one of the horses has had a slight accident, a cut foreleg. It's not that serious, I don't think, but could you come and have a look? I think it might need stitching.'

'Right, I'll be there. Straight up the Woodleigh Road, isn't it?'

Keira listened to the terse directions, her mind already busy. How come it was Daniel who had summoned her and not Fiona Barstow herself? What was Daniel doing at Fiona's so early on a Sunday morning?

Don't ask, she told herself. She doubted that he had gone over to have an early morning lesson in dressage. But it's really none of your business, she reminded herself sternly as she thought over what she needed to take. As she put down the phone there was a knock at the door. It was Jim Bishop.

'Hi Keira, you've just had Daniel's call? He phoned me first; I got it on the mobile on my way home just now. I hope you don't think I'm out of line, but I told him I'd be glad if you could do this one. I've been up half the night with a sick bull — a very valuable animal so I couldn't leave anything to chance. He'd picked up a piece of wire, so I had to operate.'

'No problem.' Keira gave him a sympathetic smile, noting the rings of tiredness under his eyes. 'You'd better get to your bed if you're going to make the barbeque later. I'd be glad to give Christine a hand if she wants, once I get back.'

'Thanks. I'm sure she'd appreciate that. Good luck with the horse.'

The directions were easy to follow and soon Keira was pulling into the gravelled yard. Daniel was standing there wearing faded blue jeans and a short-sleeved shirt that had the air of being hastily pulled on.

Keira's heart lurched at the sight of him; his hair flopping over his forehead in the way she remembered so well. He waved a hand in greeting.

'Thanks for coming so quickly. She's over here.'

'Who? Fiona?'

'No, the horse. Fiona's in the house, cooking breakfast — I told her I'd look after things out here. One of her helpers is on holiday; the other one isn't expected for another hour. By the way, your patient is Afton, the chestnut mare who ran over me.' He smiled. 'But I don't bear a grudge. If I can be any help, tell me what to do.'

Keira fell into step beside him, looking around her at the well-kept stable yard. Curious equine faces looked out of a couple of stable doors, observing their progress, and she felt a pang of longing for her own pony, Buster, now in well-deserved retirement.

Keeping her tone deliberately casual, she turned to Daniel and asked, 'Do you know what happened?'

'Took a fence too fast, from what Fiona told me. They went out for an early morning ride — Fiona often goes out first thing when the roads are quiet. The mare is highly strung and something startled her, a rabbit or something. She's gashed her foreleg, and I think it will need stitching. Fiona said to get a hose on it, so I've done that, and I think it's got the swelling down. Here she is; see what you think.'

They went inside a purpose-built stable block where the chestnut mare waited in a loose box. Keira was pleased to see that someone — probably Daniel — had secured her to a tie-up ring, always a good precaution, especially with an animal who had a reputation for being highly strung.

'All right, girl, easy now.' Keira put out a hand and ran it down the mare's smooth side. Afton sidled away and reared slightly, ears laid back, upper lip raised.

Suddenly Keira was back in the market square — the terrified horse plunging and rearing — the still figure lying on the cobbles. She closed her eyes to shut out the vision, but it remained, still potent and disturbing.

6

'Are you all right?' Daniel was at her side, his voice concerned. Keira nodded wordlessly. She couldn't trust herself to speak. She stood where she was, trying to control her near panic. It was ridiculous, she knew it was, but she just couldn't help it.

And then Daniel's arms were round her, steadying, soothing. 'I know, I understand. Don't worry about it, take your time.'

'I'm sorry.' Her words were muffled as she rested her head against the comforting wall of his chest. 'I — I can just see you lying there — '

His arms tightened round her. 'But I'm here now, right as rain. Thanks to you.' Gently he pushed her back from him and stood gazing down into her eyes, as though he wanted to add his resolve to hers. 'I can easily phone for

Chris or Greg if you want. But I think you can handle this, Keira. I know you can.'

For a few long seconds she stood looking up at him, drawing strength from him. Every instinct screamed at her to step forward into his arms, to raise her face for his kiss — but something — common sense, maybe — held her back. Then Afton whinnied, breaking the spell, and Keira snapped back to reality. She moved away from Daniel and ran her hand down the horse's neck, speaking quietly and reassuringly, banishing the bad memories.

'Come on, milady, let's see what you've been up to. What have you been doing to yourself?'

She saw straightaway what had happened; the left foreleg had a small but ugly flap of skin hanging loose. The bleeding had stopped thanks to the cold water treatment, but it was obvious that the wound should be stitched. Her veterinary training took over.

'You've done a good job,' she said to Daniel. 'When she's got used to me I'll just trim the hair around the wound and clean it up.'

She stayed beside the horse for a few more minutes, keeping up a reassuring flow of talk while she carried out a few checks. 'Can you pass me my stethoscope, please?' she asked Daniel. She pressed it against the horse's side and listened for the pulse.

'A bit raised, but I'd expect that. She's in good condition otherwise; a very fine animal, even if she nearly did break your ribs.'

'I'll forgive her that, this once.' Daniel grinned. 'It wasn't her fault and there was no malice involved, was there, old girl?'

Keira carried on, concentrating on making a neat job. At last she sat back on her heels and surveyed her handiwork with modest satisfaction.

'That's that. I won't bandage it, it should be OK. Just a couple of shots now — anti-tetanus and an antibiotic, and then that's us finished. She's been a very good girl, thanks to you keeping her entertained.'

Daniel patted Afton's sleek neck. 'Well done, Afton, my old girl. And well done to you, Keira. A very neat job. We make a great team, don't you think?'

Keira straightened up. His comment made her feel awkward, especially after the way she'd turned to him for reassurance. Would he allow her to forget that? She muttered something, stuffing things back into her bag.

'Come and have a coffee,' Daniel invited. 'Fiona will have some on.'

There was nothing else for it. Keira followed him into the pleasant bungalow that stood behind the stable yard, and into the kitchen which was filled with the smell of freshly-brewed coffee mixed with frying bacon. A woman was perched on a tall stool by the stove with her back to them, her close-cropped blonde hair outlining her neat head, her slight figure trim in linen shorts and a white shirt. She turned round in surprise when Keira came in.

'Oh, are you wanting me to settle up already? Jim usually sends an invoice.'

Keira stiffened. 'I'm not after payment. Daniel invited me in for a coffee.'

Fiona poured a coffee and passed it over in silence. She gave another one to Daniel, who sat down with it, but Keira stayed on her feet. She was plainly de trop at least as far as Fiona was concerned and she felt an overwhelming desire to get away as soon as possible. She sipped at the scaldingly-hot coffee, wondering if she dare ask for more milk. Daniel, seeing her glance around, passed the jug. 'Help yourself.'

He certainly makes himself at home here, Keira thought, remembering Christine Bishop's comment. Wonder how long this has been going on?

She poured a generous amount of milk into her mug, almost overflowing it, and making the coffee unpleasantly tepid. But at least that meant it was easy to down the lot in one go and make her escape.

'Thanks, Fiona. By the way, I assume Afton is up-to-date with her shots?'

Fiona raised an eyebrow. 'Of course.'

'Good.' Keira summoned up a polite smile. 'Well, one of us will be back to check on her tomorrow. Keep an eye on the stitches, and I expect her leg will be a bit stiff, but there shouldn't be any problems.'

Fiona said something that Keira didn't catch, and came over to take a seat at the table. She hobbled slightly, and when her lower half came into view Keira saw that her right knee was strapped up. She couldn't restrain a gasp of surprise.

'Oh, didn't you realise? Afton wasn't the only casualty.' Daniel was standing beside her and noticed her reaction. 'When the horse hit the fence, Fiona came off and landed awkwardly. She called me to come and look at her knee; she seems to have twisted it. Hopefully it will be OK with rest — in fact it's time you got off it, Ms

Barstow. Remember what I said about keeping it propped up.'

To her horror, Keira realised that her face was turning bright scarlet as she registered her mistake. Hastily, hoping that Fiona hadn't noticed, she said goodbye, then turned and left the kitchen, hurrying across the yard to her car. Daniel followed.

'You've forgotten your bag.' He held it out.

'Oh — thanks.'

He was smiling, curse him and she suspected he knew what she'd been thinking. Next moment she was sure.

'I didn't spend the night here, if that's what you thought. I arrived at half past eight in answer to Fiona's phone call.'

Keira shook her head, feeling that betraying blush colouring her face again. 'It's none of my business where you spend the night.'

There was a short silence, then Daniel said, 'Fair enough, I just didn't want you getting the wrong idea.'

'Why should that make any differ- ence to anything? Unless,' her anger stirred, 'you thought I might go blabbing all round the village that you were having an affair with Fiona Barstow.'

'Of course I didn't think that!' He glared at her for a moment, then his expression softened, and he grinned. 'Though probably half of them believe that already. I guess I just felt it was important that you knew how things stood.'

Their eyes locked and held. His meaning was all too plain.

Keira stared down at the gravel at her feet, trying to compose herself. She took a deep, steadying breath. 'Right, well thank you for that. I'd better be on my way, I said I'd help Chris. She's having a barbeque this lunchtime.'

'I know; I'm invited. I'll see you there.' There was a short silence, then abruptly Daniel leaned forward and opened the car door for her.

'Thanks.' Keira slid into the car and

dumped her bag on the passenger seat. Daniel shut the door, and with a brief wave she started the engine and moved off. It was a good few minutes before she managed to steady her jangling nerves.

How ridiculous to allow a basic physical chemistry to affect her like this! Because that's all it was. Admit it; she'd always found Daniel Grant attractive, and nothing had changed there. Unfortunately it seemed she'd not been very good about hiding her feelings, and when she'd had the moment of weakness, remembering him injured by Afton — well, he'd responded in a way that was utterly male.

So now she'd just have to let him know that she wasn't interested in any sort of relationship, other than a strictly professional one. She gripped the wheel more tightly as she made herself remember Miriam's agony when Daniel had so callously walked out on her.

She was so lost in thought that she

didn't see the sheep until she was almost upon it. Then she reacted. Her right foot hit the brake and the car slewed to a halt with a screech of tyres. The sheep leapt to the right and scrambled up a bank, then Keira saw there were others milling around further down the lane. Clearly they'd got out somehow; here could be a traffic hazard, let alone the risk to the animals themselves.

Quickly she got out of the car and stood in the roadway, arms spread wide, making shooing gestures at the sheep. 'Go on, get back there! Move, you dozy creatures.'

A figure appeared at a bend in the lane and Keira recognised Frank Kelman, one of the practice's clients. 'Miss Forrest, good to see you, love. Are you OK?' he added anxiously, seeing Keira's car at an odd angle across the road.

'I'm fine. So's the sheep, but it was a close encounter. Can I help you? How did they get out?'

The farmer's face darkened. 'Don't rightly know, but it's my belief there was a dog involved. Something panicked them at any rate and they went straight through the hedge.'

Keira caught his mood. 'That's bad. Are any of them injured?'

'Not as far as I can see. But they might well have been. Anyway, let's get them back; I'd appreciate your help if you have the time.' He whistled and a black and white collie came racing up the lane towards them. 'I've got Jed here to round them up, but it'd be good if you could go ahead and open the gate for us.'

Keira went ahead to open the gate when Jed and his master brought the sheep back along the lane. Her thoughts were troubled. If there were a dog chasing sheep it would have to be found and dealt with quickly before it did any damage to the animals or before the farmer took matters into his own hands, as he was legally entitled to do.

A vision came into her head of Finn the wolfhound, hurtling round the supermarket. Could he be the culprit? Keira bit her lip; she'd grown fond of the gangly young dog and the thought of him summarily shot for chasing sheep sent a shiver down her spine. Surely it couldn't be Finn?

She'd have to have a word with Daniel, find out if Finn was securely shut up in his run. And sooner rather than later get the obedience classes going. Oh for heaven's sake, she thought furiously, is everything conspiring to throw the two of us together?

The sheep, calmer now, came into view with Jed at their heels and Keira opened the gate to let them back into the field. Frank Kelman followed.

'Thanks, love. I'd better get on now and patch up that hedge before they're out again. Care for a cuppa with the wife? She'll soon have the kettle on.'

'No, that's fine thanks. I'm supposed to be at the Bishops for a barbeque. I'd better be getting on.'

By the time she arrived at the Bishops' the barbeque was in full swing. Jim, a butcher's apron tied round his ample waist, waved a pair of tongs at her.

'At last! What took you so long? Daniel's already here. Did you have to perform major surgery on that horse?'

'No, just a bit of suturing. What held me up was a gang of sheep loose in a lane; they were blocking the road and I helped get them back into the field.'

'Whose were they?'

'Frank Kelman's.'

'Oh.' Jim put a juicy burger on a bun and handed it to her. 'Here, get outside this. It's unlike Frank to let his stock escape. He's usually very careful about keeping his fences up to scratch.'

Keira decided to say nothing about a dog panicking the sheep into breaking through a hedge. At least not to Jim. She took advantage of her mouth being full of burger not to reply and fortunately Jim was distracted by Christine with a tray of sausages to be cooked. Keira turned to move away from the confusion and found herself facing Daniel.

'Hi. Where'd you get to?'

'I — ' A fit of coughing seized her as a piece of bun went down the wrong way. She waved an arm helplessly.

The next minute a hand slammed into her back. 'Better?'

'Agh — yes. Thanks.'

'Come and sit down. Can I get you something to drink?'

'Please. A white wine and soda would be great.'

She sat down on a garden bench while she waited for him to come back, meanwhile trying to decide what to say to someone that their dog is in danger of getting himself shot?

'Here you are.' He put a glass into her hand and sat down next to her. Instinctively she moved slightly, not wanting any contact.

'Cheers.' He raised his glass in toast and Keira, after a second's hesitation, clinked hers against it.

'That's better.' She took a deep breath. 'Daniel, there's something I wanted to say —

'Hot dog anyone?' Christine strolled over with a plate of food. 'Or a sticky drumstick for you, Keira? Paper napkins here for your fingers. What a brilliant day it's turned out to be.'

'Wonderful.' Daniel took a hot dog, and chatted animatedly to Christine while Keira waited, trying to hid her impatience. At last, as Christine moved on, he turned back to her.

'Now, where were we? You had something you wanted to say. Go on then I'm all yours.'

Keira let the irony of that remark pass. She took a swig of her drink. 'OK. It's quite serious actually; it has to be faced. It's — '

'Daniel, Daniel!' The twin sons of Daniel's medical partner, Dr Hannah Forbes rushed over. 'Look what we've got, it's a robot, you can control it — '

Keira got up. The constant interruptions were driving her mad, when all she wanted to do was satisfy herself that Finn was safely shut up and not out causing havoc amongst Farmer Kelman's sheep. If it was going to be impossible to exchange two words with Daniel without being interrupted by half the village, well, she'd damn well go and see for herself.

Leaving Daniel being shown how to work the large plastic robot, she walked quickly across the lawn and into the lane that led to his house. At the gate she looked back to see if anyone had noticed her departure, but it seemed no-one had. Predictably Daniel, now controlling the twins' robot, was the centre of attention. There was a shout of laughter as he made it whizz across the lawn, then perform a deft figure-of-eight.

Keira walked quickly down the lane. Outside Daniel's house she paused for a moment as she always did when she passed it. It was a lovely place, its thatched roof capping white-rendered walls laden with climbing roses. Their perfume surrounded her as she walked up the path, but she hadn't come to admire the grounds. She hurried round the side of the house to where she knew the run had been made to contain Finn after the supermarket incident.

The wire netting walls of the small compound seemed sturdy enough, but where was the wolfhound? The enclosure was empty.

'Finn, Finn! Where are you, boy? Here, dog!'

Keira bit her lip as she surveyed the vacant run. It was looking as though her worst suspicions were correct and Finn actually was guilty of chasing sheep. Daniel could have a real problem on his hands.

Slowly she turned and retraced her steps, her mind mulling over what to do. She was so lost in her private world that she didn't notice the figure turning the corner of the house until she walked straight into him. Strong hands grasped her elbows as she staggered and nearly fell. She gasped.

'Daniel! What are you doing here?'

He grinned down at her. 'I happen to live here. Perhaps I should put the question to you.' His fingers slid tantalisingly from her elbows down to her wrists, like a long, slow caress; his eyes held hers. 'Maybe what you want to say to me has to be said in private, is that it? Shall we go inside?'

7

Keira swallowed hard. The invitation in Daniel's eyes was real enough, she wasn't imagining it. Nor was she imagining her own response; every instinct shrieked at her to accept.

'This isn't a social call. I came to find Finn.'

'Finn? But why?'

'Because — ' Keira hesitated a moment, but then rushed on. He had to know, so there was no point in trying to be tactful. 'Because a dog has been chasing sheep. I've just come from the Kelmans' farm. From the description they gave me it might well have been Finn, and we both know that he has a bit of a reputation for escaping. I wanted to be sure it wasn't him, but when I tried to ask you about it back at the barbeque — well, I couldn't get a word in edgeways.'

She turned back to face him. 'So I decided to come down here and see for myself. And Finn's not here!'

She waited for signs of concern, but Daniel seemed unperturbed. 'It was good of you to take an interest, and I'm sorry you got a shock. But, you needn't worry, my neighbours offered to take Finn out today while I was at the barbeque. They're very attached to him.'

'You don't think he could have got away from them?'

'I'm sure he couldn't. They were taking him in their car to the seaside for a run on the beach. So there's no possibility that he could be the sheep chaser. You'll have to look elsewhere for the culprit. Maybe those so-called New Age campers up on the heath? When I drove past the other day I noticed they had one or two scrawny-looking animals hanging around.'

'Really? Perhaps we should get the RSPCA to investigate,' Keira said. She was overwhelmed with relief that Finn seemed to be exonerated, but anxious to get to the bottom of things preferably before any more sheep were attacked. 'I'll phone them first thing tomorrow.'

'Great. And now, seeing as you're here, can I invite you in for a drink? You've never seen the inside of the house yet, have you?'

Keira bit her lip. If the interior of Daniel's house was anything like as charming as the outside it would be well worth seeing, but she couldn't allow herself to accept the invitation. The less time she spent with him the better. She had to admit she was finding her promise to Miriam increasingly hard to keep.

She shook her head. 'Some other time, perhaps. I ought to be getting back to the barbeque.'

'Ah, you're worried that people might notice we're both missing, put two and two together and make five. Is that it?'

'Well, no, actually,' Keira denied hotly, even though she suspected Daniel was speaking the truth. 'I promised

Christine I'd give her a hand clearing up.'

'I see.' If he didn't believe her he diplomatically gave no sign of it. 'Well, I'd offer to help you, except that I have a phone call to make. That's why I came home, by the way, I wasn't pursuing you. A friend's hoping to visit — you might remember him from university — his name's Peter Clark.'

Keira wrinkled her brow. 'Sounds vaguely familiar.'

★ ★ ★

Keira straightened up from her examination of the purring tom cat, and smiled at his anxious owner.

'He's much better, Mrs Grainger. I think that last round of antibiotics has done the trick.'

'So it's not asthma, then?'

'I don't think so. His chest sounds perfectly clear.'

'Oh, wonderful! I'll be able to go into hospital feeling easy in my mind now.'

Gently Keira put the cat back in his carrier. 'Oh, is this to get your hip done? When are you going in?'

'At the end of this week. I was expecting to have to wait a lot longer but there's been a cancellation.'

'And have you made arrangements for all your cats?'

'Yes, my daughter's going to come and stay while I'm in hospital.'

'Great. So everything's worked out fine. Doctor Grant will be pleased you're getting the op done at last.'

'Yes, he's been badgering me about it for ages. He's a wonderful doctor, you know, Miss Forrest. We all think a lot of him round here.'

'Yes, I can see that.' Keira kept her face expressionless as she typed up a few brief notes on the computer. 'Well, all the best, Mrs Grainger, and I hope you'll be hopping around like a spring chicken next time I see you.'

They both laughed at the thought. Keira was still smiling when her next patient came in — a guinea pig carefully carried by a small, worried-looking boy, accompanied by his mother.

'Hi. What can I do for you? Oh — ' she smiled at the little boy. 'I remember you from the first time I was here. I clipped your guinea pig's teeth. She's called Hazel, isn't she?'

'Yes. I told Mum you'd remember.' The little boy looked impressed, and slightly less worried. 'I'm Mark.'

'So you are. And what's the matter with Hazel this time? Teeth OK?'

'Yes.' Mark placed Hazel on the treatment table, and Keira immediately saw that the animal couldn't move her back legs.

'Oh dear, when did this happen?'

'Well, she had babies last week, three of them, and then we noticed this yesterday. What's the matter with her?'

'Hm, it could be one of several things.' Keira carried out a gentle examination of the little animal. 'What's the bottom of her cage made of, Mark?'

Mark exchanged a glance with his

mother, then said, 'It's plastic. Does that matter?'

'It can do. Plastic's good. If it's wire, sometimes the guinea pig might get her foot caught in it, and that could cause trouble, but there's no sign of trauma — that means injury — to Hazel's legs. It could be a vitamin C deficiency; that sometimes causes this sort of paralysis. Or maybe an infection, but she looks well enough in herself and her temperature is OK. I think we'll try her with chewable vitamin C tablets, and I'll prescribe a steroid as well. If she's no better in a day or two, bring her back.'

A short while later, Daniel arrived with Finn for his first obedience lesson. 'Finn! How are you, you adorable creature!' Keira got down on her knees to greet the gangly puppy, who responded by giving her face a good lick. 'Ugh, I asked for that! He's in fine form, I can see.'

'He certainly is, and very pleased to see you.' Daniel grinned as he hauled on Finn's collar so that Keira could get up. 'I don't know how he'll feel about the obedience training though.'

'I have every confidence in him,' Keira assured Daniel solemnly. 'Lianne's here because she's interested in setting up a puppy class, so she's going to sit in on things, if that's all right with you?'

'Perfectly.'

Daniel was completely straight-faced, but Keira wondered if he suspected the truth. That she didn't want to be alone with him, even with Finn as chaperone. She put that thought to one side and turned her attention to the matter in hand.

'The first thing we have to do is get him to sit. Have you tried that at all?'

'No,' Daniel said cheerfully. 'I wouldn't have a clue where to start, and he knows it, don't you, boy?'

Finn thumped his shaggy tail.

'All right.' Keira took a dog biscuit out of the pocket of her green overall. 'We'll start at square one. Now, we work by rewarding him for what he does correctly. We never punish him for failing to do what we ask; he wouldn't understand. It's all about reinforcing good behaviour. You stand facing him, and hold the biscuit just out of reach, like this. When he lifts his head and shoulders to get the biscuit, his bottom should go down — see? And you say 'Sit!' and reward him with the biscuit and some praise. There, Finn! What a good boy!' She patted the puppy and fondled his ears. 'What a clever dog!'

'My turn now?'

'OK. Go ahead.'

But it wasn't so easy this time. Finn, maybe getting wise to what was going on, jumped up and snatched the biscuit, taking Daniel by surprise. Keira raised her eyes to heaven.

'You must be prepared for that. And only say 'sit' once. You want him to recognise the single word.'

It took a lot of effort and repetition, plus a lot of patience on Keira's part before she began to sense a breakthrough. 'I think he's getting the idea, don't you, Lianne? The important thing now is for you to keep practising at home. Next time we'll try getting him to stay.'

'I'd hoped we might try that tonight,' Daniel said hopefully.

'No way, it would only confuse him. We can't go too fast. How is he on the lead?'

'Not bad. Want to try him?'

'Yes, let's take him outside. You have him, Lianne.'

Lianne clipped the lead on to Finn's collar and they went outside into the courtyard.

All went well at first, and Keira was beginning to feel quite hopeful, until Finn spotted a cat. He was off like a flash, barking furiously, wrenching the leash out of Lianne's hand.

'Finn! Bad boy!'

Keira sprinted after him, followed by Daniel, who managed to grab the trailing lead, just as the outraged cat sprang up on to a stone wall.

'Oh dear,' Daniel commented wearily.

'It looks like we still have some way to go.'

'You can't get there all at once,' Keira said. 'At least we've made progress with getting him to sit. Don't let him forget that.'

'I won't,' Daniel promised. 'Perhaps we should call it a day for now.'

'I think so. Thanks for your help, Lianne.'

She expected Daniel to take Finn away, but to her surprise he stayed put. 'Have you a moment, Keira?'

'Sure, what is it? Something the matter with Finn?'

'No, nothing like that. Just a small confession.'

'A what?'

'I don't think you're going to like this.' He flashed her an apologetic smile. Out of the corner of her eye Keira noticed Lianne walking away, clearly feeling that Daniel had something private to communicate. She began to feel slightly panicky.

'I was speaking to Mrs Grainger this

afternoon. She phoned me up in a tizzy, wanting to pull out of her hip operation, and, well, to cut a long story short, I've volunteered you — and me — to help look after her cats.'

'What!'

Daniel went on quickly. 'She was on the verge of refusing point blank to go into hospital. Apparently her daughter isn't very good with cats, and one — Fred, I think it was — has taken a very definite dislike to the poor girl. Anyway, I was so desperate to get Mrs G into hospital before she could change her mind that I said you and I would keep an eye on the cats. She has a very high opinion of you, you know.'

Keira was horrified. 'Do you make a habit of volunteering people for things without their knowledge?'

'Well, no — '

'Then why start with me? Next thing I know, half my clients will be expecting me to keep an eye on their pets for them.'

'I take your point, and I'm sorry, but

I thought you'd be happy to do it this once. After all, this is a special case. Don't you understand?'

Keira sighed. 'I suppose I do. And if Mrs Grainger is expecting us to do it, then I don't have much choice, do I? But, oh Lordy, I'm not particularly keen on meeting Fred again. Last time we met I narrowly avoided having my eyes scratched out. And I can't help thinking that he's the cat Finn just chased. That will give him another grudge against us.'

'Let's hope he's forgotten all about that,' Daniel said, optimistically. 'Anyhow, our services might not be needed. Mrs G's daughter might get on better than her mother expects.'

'I hope so,' Keira replied, with feeling.

'Fingers crossed then. Right, well, no doubt I'll see you around at work. Thanks for doing the class, we really appreciate it, don't we, Finn?'

With that, Daniel departed, Finn trotting trustingly at his side. Keira watched them go down the road. They made a good pair, she thought, the tall, lean man and the young long-legged wolfhound. When Finn grew up he would be a very good-looking dog, and of course, Daniel was —

Oh, stop it! she told herself fiercely. Remember what he did to Miriam!

★ ★ ★

She didn't see anything of Daniel the following day, and there was no summons to attend any of Mrs Grainger's cats. The daughter seemingly was coping well.

'Penny for them, Keira!' Christine Bishop's voice broke into her thoughts as they sat together over a coffee in the staff room.

'Oh, nothing in particular.'

'So you weren't wondering who to go with to the Rotary Club dinner dance?'

'The what?'

'Don't say you haven't heard of it? It's next month, one of the social highlights of the village calendar. I did think a certain GP might be planning to ask you — '

'Christine! You're not still at that matchmaking game, are you? I thought I told you, I've no wish to get tied down.'

'Mmm, quite the career woman, aren't we? No need to be touchy; it's only a dance.'

'Well, if you're hinting that Daniel might have asked me, I'm sorry to disappoint you. He hasn't.'

She finished her coffee, then deliberately changed the subject to the case of a pig with erysipelas. All the same, she couldn't help her thoughts turning to the dinner dance. Was Daniel planning to ask her to it? Or had he already asked Fiona Barstow?

After a few days had passed she still had heard nothing from Daniel about the dinner dance. By now she was convinced that he must have asked Fiona. Hardly surprising, she thought, because clearly he had got the message that she didn't want to get involved with him. She should be congratulating herself on her success, rather than feeling bereft. And she was even a touch disappointed that Mrs Grainger's daughter hadn't called them in to help with the cats.

After a tiring day that only ended at eight o'clock, she was looking forward to a quiet evening in. She made herself an omelette and settled down to eat it in front of the television, but she was scarcely half way through it when the phone rang. With a groan, remembering she was on call, she picked it up.

'Hello, Keira Forrest here.'

'Hello, Miss Forrest, it's Frank Kelman. I'm calling to tell you we've had trouble with a dog chasing sheep again.'

'Oh no.' Keira pushed away her plate. 'Any animals hurt?'

'None of the sheep, no.' He paused, and Keira sensed he was holding something back.

'What is it, Frank?'

'Well, we won't be having any more of a problem. We've shot the dog.'

'Oh dear. But you're within your rights, no need to worry about it. Do you know whose it is?'

'I'm afraid I do, Miss Forrest.' The farmer's voice was heavy. 'It's that wolfhound puppy of the doctor's.'

8

Keira drew in a deep calming breath. She didn't want to believe what she was hearing. Not quite sure whether she could trust her voice, she asked, 'Arc — are you certain?'

'As certain as I can be. He was always getting out, you know, and I had my suspicions from the start. I'm sorry, love, but it had to be done. Those sheep are our livelihood, and more than that, we care about their welfare.'

'I understand.' She swallowed hard. 'Where is he?'

'Lying in the field, just where he fell. I went to make sure he was dead, and then that's when I realised whose dog it was. I tried to phone the doctor, but there was no reply, just an answering machine. I didn't like to leave that sort of message on it, so I phoned you, knowing you and he were friendly, like.'

Keira let that pass. Tears were pricking at her eyelids as she thought of the friendly, boisterous, wolfhound puppy. If only they had done more — sooner — to train him. If only Daniel had taken more care to make the run escape-proof. If only, if only —

Somehow she found her voice. 'Thanks for letting me know, Frank. I'll tell Doctor Grant, don't worry about that. Could you bring Finn in from the field?' There was a catch in her throat, but she went on, 'I don't like to think of him lying out there.'

'I'll do that, love. And I'm very sorry about what's happened.'

'Thanks.'

Keira put the phone down, and sat back, eyes unfocused. Poor, poor Finn! And poor Daniel — how was he going to react when he heard this news?

Her fingers went to the phone again, but she hesitated. Frank Kelman was right; this wasn't the sort of news you should pass on in a telephone call, much less leave on an answering machine. The best way of doing it was in person, even though it was much more difficult.

It was a chilly, wet evening; autumn was drawing in. It suited Keira's mood as, blinking back tears, she picked up a jacket and went out.

There was a light on in Daniel's house. She walked up the path, mentally rehearsing what she was going to say. But first she wanted to be absolutely certain. She walked round the corner of the house to Finn's run. It was empty, so there could be no mistake.

Hoping against hope, she called his name softly. 'Finn! Finn, here boy!'

But no familiar shape appeared in the shadows. Heavy-hearted, Keira walked up to the door of the house and knocked. A trickle of rain ran down her cheeks — or was it tears? She pulled up her collar against the freshening breeze and waited.

There was no reply. Daniel must have left the light on by accident, or maybe as a security precaution. Keira bit her lip, wondering what to do next.

Perhaps the best thing to do was go out to the farm and take a look at Finn. There was just a chance — the smallest possible, she had to admit — that there might be something she could do. She set off down the path to go back for her car.

Just as she reached the gate, another car drew up and she recognised it as Daniel's. She ran forward and wrenched the door open.

'Daniel! Have you got Finn with you?'

'No. I've just been retrieving one of Mrs Grainger's cats from a tree. You'd never believe the trouble I had — ' he stopped, suddenly registering her expression. 'Why? What's the matter?'

Suddenly she couldn't hold back the tears any longer. They welled up and spilled over her cheeks. 'I'm sorry — I'm so sorry — '

'Here, get in the car out of the rain.' Daniel reached out and gently took her arm, guiding her into the seat. He picked up a box of tissues and handed it to her. 'What's happened to upset you?'

He was being so kind, it just made things worse. She was going to have to give him this ghastly news.

She wiped her eyes and, praying that her voice would last out, she told him. 'Finn got out. He's been chasing sheep. And — oh, Daniel, there's no easy way to tell you this — the farmer shot him.'

Silence wrapped itself around them, broken only by the patter of rain on the car roof. Daniel stared blankly. 'I don't understand,' he said at last. 'There must be some mistake.'

Keira shook her head. 'I'm afraid not. The farmer was very definite. I'm so sorry — '

And then she couldn't hold the tears back any longer. She put her hands to her face and sobbed.

Then, very gently, she felt Daniel's arms round her, gathering her to him, his hand cradling her head. She rested her cheek on the firm wall of his chest, making no attempt to pull away. It felt completely right.

His voice was gruff when he eventually spoke. 'Should we go out there now?'

'If you want to. It's Frank Kelman's place.'

'Fine.'

They drove in silence, and soon pulled up outside the farm. Frank Kelman came hurrying out to meet them.

'Doctor Grant. So Miss Forrest managed to contact you, then. I'm sorry about this, it's a bad business.'

'I know, Frank.' Daniel got out and leaned against the car. 'I'm willing to compensate you for any injuries to your sheep — '

'No need. They got a fright, but there's no damage done. And there won't be any more danger to them — now.'

Keira got out of the car and came round to Daniel. As they crossed the yard behind the farmer, it seemed the natural thing to do to reach for his hand. His fingers closed round hers and gripped them tightly.

They entered a barn, dimly lit by one bulb. At their feet lay a pathetic shaggy bundle. Keira knelt to examine it. Her heart thudded.

'Daniel, I don't think — '

Daniel, who had been standing with the farmer, swiftly came over. 'What is it?'

'It's not Finn.'

* * *

Later, in the farm kitchen, over a mug of steaming hot tea, the true picture emerged.

'I left him with the neighbours,' Daniel explained, 'because it was such a wretched night. His run isn't completely waterproof. But when you turned up, so distraught, I assumed you'd seen them and he'd somehow managed to escape from their house. I never thought to question you.'

'And I never thought to ask,' Keira said. 'Once I'd seen the empty run, I put two and two together — '

'And made five.' Daniel smiled at her as they both remembered the last time he'd spoken those words. Things were very different now.

As he put his arm round her and drew her close to him, Keira caught the approving glance of Mrs Kelman, and smiled to herself. So maybe they were fulfilling the expectations of the entire community, but so what?

'So that poor beast must belong to the New Age traveller folk?' Farmer Kelman suggested.

'I think so. The RSPCA have already been out and warned them about the state of their dogs. They may be prosecuted over this, or have their other animals taken away and re-homed.'

'That would be no bad thing,' the farmer commented. 'Give them a new start in life, like that dog of yours. I'm sorry I suspected him, Doctor.'

130

'No problem,' Daniel said, smiling. 'He's not been the best-behaved of dogs, I'll admit. But all that's set to change because the vet here has got him in hand.'

'I'm glad to hear that,' Mrs Kelman put in. 'And maybe there'll be other changes, too.'

'Maybe,' Daniel agreed, and the expression in his eyes as he glanced at Keira was unmistakable.

The atmosphere as they drove back to the village was very different from the journey out.

'I'd like to stop off at the neighbours,' Daniel said, 'and pick Finn up. I want to satisfy myself that he's all right.'

'Me, too,' Keira said. 'I've never been so anxious to set eyes on him.'

'I know. Oh, and Keira — '

'Yes?'

'I wondered if you might be free the last Saturday in this month? It's the Rotary Club dinner dance, and I thought you might like to go. I've been meaning to ask for a while.'

Keira squeezed his arm mischievously. 'I thought you were never going to get round to it. I'd love to come.'

He slanted her a delighted smile. 'Wonderful. But that's a bit far-off. How about dinner for two tomorrow night? They say The Feathers at Ashford do a good meal.'

'That would be lovely.'

'And by the way — ' He was suddenly serious. 'I'd like to take that opportunity to sort a few things out.'

'You mean the business about Miriam, I suppose?'

'Yes. A lot of things happened that I very much regret and I'd like to try to put things straight. Would you mind?'

'Of course not.' Keira didn't hesitate. It was only fair that she should hear Daniel's side of the story at long last.

Later Daniel dropped Keira off at her flat, leaving her more contented than she had been for a good while. His goodnight kiss was warm on her lips as she hurried up the stairs and let herself in. She hugged her arms round her waist, marvelling at the way things had turned out; Finn was safe and well, and had been exuberantly pleased to see them, and in addition to that, it looked as though she and Daniel might have a future together.

The next day even the presence of Fred, her least favourite cat, in the surgery did nothing to dampen her mood.

'His eyes are very red and sore-looking,' Mrs Grainger's daughter explained, holding the growling cat gingerly.

'Let's have a look at him.' With Lianne's help, Keira examined Fred who hissed a warning at her. Plainly he remembered their last encounter.

'It's not too bad,' Keira said, several minutes and one scratched hand later. 'Just a touch of conjunctivitis. I'll give you some drops for it, although I don't know how easy it will be for you to get them in. Fred isn't exactly the most co-operative cat I've ever encountered.'

'Oh. Would you — might you be able

to come and do them for me? Mum's very good at that sort of thing, but I'm not, I'm afraid.'

Keira sighed inwardly. 'All right,' she conceded. 'I'll put one in now and then I'll be round some time this evening. How is Mrs Grainger, by the way?'

'Oh, she's fine.' The daughter's face brightened up as she watched Keira insert the drops into Fred's eyes. 'She's had the op and she's desperate to get out. Any day now I should think.'

'We'll see if we can get Fed back to rights before she sees him. It shouldn't take long to clear this up.'

At the end of the morning, Keira went back to her flat for a bite of lunch before she started her farm visits. As she ate a sandwich, she opened the wardrobe to pick out a dress for that evening's date with Daniel. Not too formal — it was only supper in a pub — but comfortable and flattering. As she was making her decision the bleep of the answering machine reminded her she had a message. Better check it first in case it was urgent.

She quickly finished the sandwich and pressed the button. To her shock, Miriam's voice greeted her.

'Surprise! I'm in your part of the world today, at a seminar. I wondered if I could borrow a bed for the night or even a sofa. I'd love to get together for a chat and see if this place of yours matches up to your description of it. I'll depend on you to keep you-know-who off the scene. Give me a call if it's not convenient. Bye.'

Keira ran a hand through her hair in sudden horrified frustration. Miriam had always been impulsive, but really! She'd have to cancel the visit, or postpone it. The sooner the better.

She rang Miriam's mobile number, but her annoyance grew as she found her phone was switched off. How like Miriam! To make an arrangement just out of the blue, assuming everyone would fit in. Now what was she going to do?

There was only one thing for it. She

picked up the phone again and rang Daniel.

'Daniel Grant.'

'Hi, it's me.' She went on quickly, before she could have second thoughts. 'I'm terribly sorry but we'll have to re-schedule tonight. Something's cropped up.'

'Oh. That's a pity. Anything serious?'

Keira considered this briefly. She was on the brink of telling him the whole truth but something stopped her. The last thing she wanted was for him to come round and attempt to explain things to Miriam. There would prob-ably be an awful scene which would upset everyone and achieve nothing. 'No,' she said firmly. 'Not serious, but time-consuming.'

'And more important than a mere dinner date.'

He sounded ever so slightly miffed, but Keira couldn't help that. It didn't stop her feeling very guilty though as she once again gave her apologies then said goodbye. She went out on her farm visits with a heavy heart.

Miriam declared herself enchanted with the flat. 'The view is fantastic! And I love these sloping ceilings — so quaint! What a marvellous place — if only a certain person didn't live in the neighbourhood. That must be a real downer for you.'

'Well — ' Keira hesitated. Why did life have to be so difficult? 'How about a glass of wine?' she suggested, cross with herself for putting off the evil moment when she'd have to tell Miriam about her new relationship with Daniel. How did you explain to someone that you'd cold-bloodedly broken a promise?

While she went to the fridge to get the chilled white wine, she rehearsed what she was going to say. She jumped when the doorbell rang and heard Miriam call, 'I'll get that.'

Keira glanced out of the window, and her mouth went dry. Daniel's car was standing in the stable yard.

'It's OK, Miriam.' The wine bottle

slipped from her fingers and crashed to the floor, but she ignored it and ran through. She was too late. Daniel and Miriam were staring at each other across the threshold.

Daniel recovered first. 'Hi, Miriam, how're things?' Without waiting for a reply, he glanced over at Keira and his expression was bleak. 'Sorry to disturb you. I just wanted to make sure everything was all right.'

He handed over a bottle of wine he'd been carrying. 'You might like to have this while you chat about old times.'

He turned on his heel and went off down the stairs. After a moment's frenzied silence, Keira set off after him. She caught him up just as he reached his car.

'Daniel! Hang on a minute.'

'Why? You're surely not going to invite me up.'

'No, but — '

'It's OK.' His eyes were hard. 'You couldn't waste any time, could you, in getting her over for a girlie chat? So you

138

could tell her how you'd got me strung along, and you could both have a good laugh? Well, don't let me disappoint you.'

Before she could say anything he was in his car and accelerating away. Keira stood looking after him for a minute, then slowly she went back inside.

Miriam was in the kitchen, clearing up the broken bottle of wine Keira had dropped. She was ominously silent.

'I was going to explain — ' Keira began.

'No need. I should have expected it, really.' Miriam dropped the glass fragments into the rubbish bin with a clatter. 'He's a very attractive man. As I know to my cost.'

'I know that, and don't think I don't sympathise. But it was a long time ago.'

'I can't forget. I took an overdose because of what he did to me.'

'Yes, yes. But we were all younger then, less experienced. People change.'

'I don't believe I'm hearing this!' Miriam's voice rose, and she hurried through to the hallway where her overnight bag was lying. 'Well, I'm not stopping here if that's the way you feel. There must be a hotel somewhere nearby.'

'Oh, Miriam, can't we discuss this calmly? Like civilised, grown-up people?'

'I'm sorry.' Miriam was pulling on her coat. 'Where that man is concerned, calmness doesn't enter into it. My whole life has been ruined by him. I could have been a qualified doctor by now if it wasn't for him.'

'But you're successful in what you do now,' Keira tried. 'Maybe your change of career was a positive step.'

Miriam cast her a withering glance. 'He's really got to you, hasn't he? I bet he's only doing it to get back at me.'

Keira gasped. 'Miriam, that's preposterous! He wouldn't do a thing like that!'

'Wouldn't he? I'd believe anything of that man.'

Keira said nothing. Miriam was in such a state there was no point in trying to reason with her. She took a deep, slow breath.

'Well, if you're determined to go, there's a good motel on the Steadham Road. It's about four miles, you can't miss it.'

'Thanks.'

'And look, I'm really, really sorry about all this. I didn't mean any of it to happen.'

Miriam didn't reply. She gathered up her things and left the flat, her face set. A couple of minutes later, Keira heard her hire car drawing out of the yard. Slowly, she went through to the kitchen and finished mopping up the spilled wine. It looked like she'd just lost a friend, she couldn't imagine Miriam forgiving her for this.

And, more importantly, it looked as though her budding relationship with Daniel Grant was over as soon as it had begun.

9

Keira took the coward's way out and sent Daniel a brief note, telling him that she wouldn't be able to partner him to the dinner dance after all. For his part he seemed to be spending as little time in and around the medical centre as he possibly could. Certainly he never put in an appearance in the coffee room that the vets shared with the GPs.

Keira was relieved. She felt terrible about what had happened. But maybe, she told herself in an attempt at optimism, maybe this proves that Miriam was right. Seeing her again made Daniel realise how badly he'd behaved. Probably I'm best out of that relationship, it was too risky.

Hold on to that idea, she thought. In time you might come to believe it.

Jim Bishop was the first to notice her

change of mood. 'What's up, Keira?' he asked in his typically down-to-earth fashion. 'You look like a wet Thursday in November. It's actually a very pleasant September morning and you're depressing us all.'

'Sorry Jim.' Keira had to smile. 'I don't mean to be a wet blanket, I'm just a bit preoccupied.'

'Hmm. Planning what to wear for the dance, I'll be bound. Christine has been going around looking just as miserable. The only thing that'll cure her is for me to get my wallet out and send her off to Steadham to buy a new dress. Perhaps you should go together.'

Keira shook her head. 'I'm not needing a new dress, Jim. I'm not going to the dance.'

'Not going! But I thought you and Daniel — '

Lianne, sitting nearby, made a shushing sound. Word had got out that there was a rift between Keira and Daniel, but it had evidently not reached Jim and he ignored Lianne's efforts.

'What is all this? You can't have fallen out already?'

'Let's say we've agreed we're not right for each other.' Keira got up and went through to the dispensary. There was no-one there and she started looking through the latest consignments of drugs, hoping that Jim would not follow her.

She was disappointed. 'Keira, are you sure about this? Is there nothing I can do to help? Have a word with Daniel, maybe — '

Keira whirled round. 'No, Jim! You mustn't say anything! Please don't interfere.'

She bit down hard on her lower lip, willing herself not to give way to her emotions. Jim stared at her for a long moment, then shook his head sadly.

'Women! I'll never understand them, even after nearly twenty years of marriage. All right, love, I won't stick my great oar in. But, remember, if you ever want someone to talk to, or a shoulder to cry on, then Christine and I are always available.'

'Thanks, Jim.' Keira forced a smile. He was a good sort, was Jim, one of the best. She couldn't have wished for a better employer.

'What a pity,' he was saying. 'Us vets are going to be very under-represented. There's Greg now, saying he's not going to make it either, because his fiancée can't make it down from Arbroath.' He stopped suddenly and turned to her, a smile visible beneath his bushy beard. 'Now, there's an idea — '

'Jim, don't even think about it! It's just not on!'

'Why not? I know that Greg would love to go to the dance, especially as he's persuaded them to do a 'Strip The Willow' and some other Scottish dances and you want to go, don't you? So bingo! The two of you go together. No-one will get the wrong idea. Problem is solved.'

Keira sighed. It was all too easy to get

145

swept away by Jim's breezy logic. 'I'll think about it,' she promised.

With luck, she thought, he'd forget about it and Greg might well decide to go up to Arbroath for the weekend rather than go to the dance. She could always go home to her parents; she hadn't seen them in ages. She decided to give them a ring.

'Oh darling,' her mother's voice sounded crestfallen. 'It's always lovely to see you, but that weekend just isn't possible, I'm afraid. We've booked a couple of days in Paris, on the spur of the moment. Now we're both retired there are these wonderful cheap deals. But do come some other time. How about next weekend instead?'

'Fine.' Keira felt slightly guilty about trying to use her parents as a hideaway. Serve her right that it hadn't worked, but a weekend away from the practice would be a good break. She chatted to them for a few minutes, then put the phone down, wondering what to do next.

There was a knock on the door and she went to answer it, half-apprehensive, half-hopeful that it might be Daniel, come to apologise and set things straight. But it wasn't; it was Greg.

'Hi, come in.' She held the door wide, hoping he hadn't noticed the disappointment in her face when she'd seen who it was. He grinned at her and came in.

'Hello, Keira, how are you? I can't stay long, I have to get out to inoculate some pigs.'

'Poor you. A messy business usually.'

'Can be. I'll go straight in the shower when I get back. Actually, there was something I wanted to ask you.' He looked suddenly rather embarrassed and Keira's heart sank as she realised what his request was likely to be.

She was right.

'Would you like to come to the dinner dance with me? Morag can't make it and Jim did say that you wouldn't be going with Daniel after all. Ach,' he looked away. 'I'm sorry to hear that you and he aren't getting along well.'

Keira started to frame an excuse, but Greg was still speaking.

'I thought the two of you were ideal for each other. And then the next thing I hear is he's taking that Fiona Barstow to the dance. I was fair scunnered.'

The words hit Keira like a thunderbolt. 'What was that?'

'What? Scunnered? Ach it's an old Scots word, sorry. I was — '

'No, not that. You said something about Daniel Grant taking Fiona Barstow to the dinner dance.

'Yes. She lost no time in getting her claws into him, that one. Mind you,' he went on reflectively, 'she's a good-looking girl, with her own business. A man could do worse.'

Keira was silent for a moment, mulling over what Greg had said. Well, if Daniel could get over things as quickly as that maybe she'd been overestimating the seriousness of their relationship. So, why shouldn't she go

148

to the dance with Greg? Stop being cowardly, she told herself and get out there.

She smiled at her colleague. 'All right then. If you're sure Morag doesn't mind you taking someone else, I'd be happy to go along with you. Thanks.'

★　★　★

She had to remind herself of her resolve when she and Greg took their seat at the dinner table almost opposite Daniel and Fiona. Whoever had organised the seating hadn't been aware of the situation.

Daniel greeted her and Greg with a brief smile, before turning back to attend to Fiona, who was speaking animatedly about horses and didn't bother to notice Keira and Greg.

Sitting next to Daniel were another couple and Keira found the man's face vaguely familiar. When he intercepted her glance he smiled and leaned over the table.

'Keira Forrest isn't it? I'd have recognised you anywhere.'

'Yes, I'm Keira. And I recognise your face, but I can't put a name to you.' She coloured up with mild embarrassment, then suddenly she remembered. 'You're Peter Clark, aren't you. You were the year above Daniel in the medical school.'

'That's right. And this is my wife, Julie; she was a nurse at the local hospital. Now she's fully-fledged Sister.'

'Pleased to meet you.' Keira introduced Greg, not particularly bothered about whether the Clarks took the two of them for a couple. She was pleased they were there; it gave her someone to chat to about old times. Greg's conversation, she had become depressingly aware, was strictly work related.

After the meal the tables were pushed back and the band took the stage. Peter Clark beckoned to Keira. 'Care for the first dance?'

She hesitated. 'What about Julie?'

'She's been claimed by Daniel. His

partner's not dancing, she has a bad knee apparently. So, may I have the pleasure?'

'Surely.'

Keira stood up and stepped into Peter's light hold. He was a good dancing partner, more secure than she was and it was easy to follow his lead. He was very chatty too, she soon found out.

'I'd always put you down as the quiet type back at university,' he said, 'but you're pretty talkative now. Maybe it was because that friend of yours, what was she called? Miriam, I think — anyway, she did all the talking. You never got a word in edgeways.'

Keira felt slightly uncomfortable at hearing Miriam mentioned. She looked around for Daniel, but he was partnering Julie at the other side of the room and couldn't possibly overhear.

'Yes, she was very outgoing,' she agreed, then changed the subject. 'So what are you doing now?'

'I'm a psychoanalyst. Fascinating

career. I tried to get Daniel to consider it, but he was determined to bury himself in the country.'

'He's very well thought of round here,' Keira countered. 'He's certainly made a success of his career choice.'

'I don't doubt it. There was a time though when we thought he was going to crack up and throw the whole thing away. Do you remember? You must do, because it was all because of that wretched friend of yours. Oh, I'm sorry, you might still be good pals. I can't think you would be though, after what she did to Daniel.'

Keira pulled away and stared up into his face. 'What do you — ' There was a burst of applause, the dance had ended. Peter was already thanking her for partnering him and looking around to claim his wife for the next dance. Before she could go after him, Keira felt her arm caught by Greg.

'Keira, it's the 'Dashing White Sergeant'. You know how to do this one, don't you? If we get Jim on the floor that makes our threesome.'

He didn't wait for a reply, but propelled her forward, to where Jim had already assembled Christine and — oh horror — Daniel and the veterinary nurse, Lianne. Keira consoled herself with the thought that the nature of the dance meant that she wouldn't see much of Daniel. But to her chagrin, she found herself in the middle of Greg and Daniel.

How she got through the dance she couldn't say. Daniel was a good dancer, surprisingly light-footed for such a tall man, but he made no attempt at conversation. She was bursting with questions that Peter's comments had aroused, but she knew it was pointless to seek answers from Daniel.

As soon as the dance ended she went off in search of Peter. He was nowhere to be seen. At last she ran him to earth outside the front door of the hotel, where he was indulging in a cigarette. He looked round guiltily when he saw her.

'A terrible habit, I know, but I'm trying to cut down.' He stubbed it out with his toe. 'Has Julie sent you to spy on me?'

'No, I've just come to get some fresh air.' It was partly the truth; the atmosphere was very hot inside the room as dancers gyrated round to the strains of 'YMCA'. 'I was interested to hear what you were saying about Miriam.'

She wondered if Peter would be reluctant to talk, but he seemed quite the reverse. 'Poor girl. I often wonder what happened to her.'

'She's done all right. She's the PA to a vice-president of one of the big oil firms.'

'But I'll bet she hasn't settled down with a husband or steady boyfriend?'

'No she hasn't.'

'It figures.'

Keira wondered what he meant. She also felt vaguely uncomfortable about discussing Miriam, but she felt she had to get to know the story from another angle.

She waited for a few moments, then Peter went on. 'She had Daniel right where she wanted him, you know. She even took him home to meet her parents, claiming they were engaged. Imagine his shock when he was introduced as the future son-in-law and had to listen to them talking about wedding plans and marquees in the garden and what have you. Poor old Daniel didn't know what to do. He even told me he was considering settling down with her at one point, but he couldn't do it. He decided it was only fair to tell her he just didn't feel for her in that sort of way.'

'Why didn't he?' Keira's mouth was dry.

'He was in love with someone else. I never did know who, he wouldn't tell me, but I do know that she was involved elsewhere and he didn't want to spoil things for her. So he went off to Africa to get over it.'

'And left Miriam in the lurch!'

'In the lurch? How come? It was the

only way he could end things — what else could he do? She'd built up the relationship out of nothing. Would you believe it, she even faked a suicide attempt to get him to stay. Thank God he never knew about that at the time; he was already out of the country.'

'The attempt was a fake?' Keira could hardly believe what she was hearing.

'Sure. The psychologist who treated her was my tutor at the time. He organised treatment for her and thankfully she seemed to get over it. We made sure no word of that got to Daniel; he'd have been straight back from Africa I've no doubt.'

Keira walked a few steps away, trying to come to terms with what she'd just heard. Could Peter be lying about all this? But why should he; he had nothing to gain from it. And neither did Daniel. It was plain from his behaviour towards her that he had no wish to continue their brief relationship.

Oh what a mess, she thought bleakly.

If only I'd tried to get him to talk about Miriam before now. But I didn't want to bring the subject up; I just wanted to push the whole thing under the mat and forget about it.

She turned back to Peter and pasted on what she hoped was a bright smile. 'Shall we go back inside? Your wife will be thinking you've smoked a whole pack of cigarettes by now.'

He grinned. 'Can't have that. Maybe you'd favour me with the next dance?'

As she circled the floor with Peter, Keira's mind was working overtime. She simply had to speak to Daniel. She desperately wanted him to know that she had heard his side of the story and she was gradually becoming convinced he was in the right.

But at the end of the dance she was claimed by Greg again.

'Come on, it's a 'Strip The Willow'. We have to show them how to do it. Do you know it Orcadian style?'

'What?'

He proceeded to whirl her off her

feet in a mad frenzy of a dance that had Jim Bishop whooping and hollering with delight. When at last it ended, Keira, breathless and hot, sank into a chair and gratefully poured herself a glass of water.

'That's one way to keep fit! You did very well for a beginner, Jim.'

'Ah, I've attempted it before. I'm not up to Greg's standards though.'

Keira looked around. 'Where's Daniel?'

'He's gone. Fiona said her knee was bothering her — it's been giving her trouble ever since she had that fall, remember? Anyway, Daniel's run her home.'

'Oh.' Keira had a brief unwelcome vision of Fiona and Daniel locked in each other's arms, then hastily distracted herself. Maybe it was just as well she didn't try to talk to him right then. There'd be other opportunities.

Monday morning found her back at work, her first port of call out at Kelman's farm.

'Morning, Miss Forrest,' the farmer

greeted her. 'Better day today.'

'Yes. It's cold, but at least it's dry. How's the patient?'

'Bad-tempered, I'm afraid to say,' Frank Kelman told her. Keira's heart sank. She was coming to repair a crack in the hoof of Frank's prize Friesian bull, aptly named Tyson. He was a huge animal with an uncertain disposition and it had taken a while before Keira had been able to persuade Greg and Jim that she could be trusted to deal with the creature.

'Have you got him in the pen?' she asked.

'That we have and he's tied up ready for you. Me and Bill will be there to give you a hand with him.'

'It should be straightforward enough,' Keira said hopefully.

'I hope so, love, but that hoof's giving him some pain. He can hardly bear to stand on it and you know what his temper's like at the best of times. He's in one foul mood, I warn you.'

As they neared the pen a ferocious

bellow rang out and there was the sound of angry stamping. 'He knows something's up,' Frank Kelman said. 'Are you sure you can handle this, love? I can easy send for Mr Bishop or Mr McKenzie if you like.'

'No, there's no need.' Keira's professional pride was aroused. 'I'm sure I'll be fine with your help.'

She blinked as she entered the pen. She'd forgotten just how big Tyson was. One little black eye gleamed wickedly at her as she approached and he tossed his huge head irritably.

Hoping she sounded confident, she said to Frank, 'Can you hold his head at that side, and you, Bill, at the other please. Its his left rear hoof, yes?'

She knelt down in the straw, being careful not to make any sudden movement. As she crouched there, running her hands over the hoof, her mind went back to that Sunday morning at the riding school, when she'd knelt in the straw beside Afton, with Daniel holding the horse's head.

The memory was unbelievably poignant; in a swift automatic gesture she raised a hand and pushed back her heavy fringe of hair.

Tyson, unnerved by the abrupt action, tensed suddenly. With ferocious violence, his hoof slammed into the side of Keira's head and her world exploded into a thousand pinpoints of light as she felt herself propelled across the bullpen. Then she connected sickeningly with the concrete wall and everything went black.

★   ★   ★

From far off Keira heard a voice calling her name. It was Daniel. She smiled to herself, knowing it was a dream. She didn't want to wake up to the real world where Daniel was cold and distant. Slowly she whispered his name. 'Daniel, Daniel — ' And then she drifted back to sleep.

It was very different when she did wake up. There were bright lights, smooth white blankets, and a white-coated figure shining lights into her eyes. She struggled to sit up but the world swam round drunkenly and she sank back with a groan.

'Where am I? What's happened?'

Someone put an arm round her and straightened the pillow. A woman's voice spoke reassuringly. 'You're in hospital love, with a big lump on the side of your head. You've had an encounter with a bull and come off worse.'

'Oh, I remember. Tyson.'

'Was that his name? Sounds as if he lives up to it.'

Keira opened her eyes again and tried to focus. She made out a cheerful face above a blue nurse's uniform.

'So he kicked me?' She grimaced. 'I'll never live this down. Jim and Greg will never let me treat farm animals again.'

'Don't you worry about that,' the nurse said encouragingly. 'You won't be treating any animals for a while yet, though, when you're a bit more chirpy, I'd like to ask you about my little girl's hamster. It's been off its food for a couple of days and — '

'Now nurse.' Someone in a dark blue uniform had come up. 'Keira is in no fit state to give consultations. How are you, my dear?'

'A bit muzzy,' Keira confessed. 'And my head hurts. What have I done to it?'

'You? Nothing. Pity the same can't be said for that brute of an animal.'

'He's not a brute, just a bit short-tempered. And it was my fault, I remember now. I made a sudden movement.'

'Well, for whatever reason he caught you a nasty blow on the side of the head. Had you out cold. But the good news is that the X-ray has revealed there's no fracture there. You've just got concussion.'

'Like Finn,' Keira murmured.

'Like what?'

'Oh nothing. Just a dog I once

treated. When can I go home?'

'Well, we'll be keeping you in overnight for observation. That's standard practice. Then — well, I don't know. Have you any one at home to look after you?'

'I live on my own,' Keira answered. 'But the flat's above the surgery — I live over the shop, so to speak. So I'm sure that people could pop up to see me from time to time.'

'Hmm, I don't know. We'll have to ask the doctor about that.'

The word 'doctor' triggered a thought in Keira's mind. 'Has a doctor been to see me?'

'Of course. Our SHO, Doctor Christie was here just a few minutes ago testing your reflexes. We'll see what she has to say about discharging you tomorrow.'

'Oh, I didn't mean her. I meant as a visitor.'

'You haven't had any visitors yet, dear. You're in no fit state.'

'Oh I see.'

Keira closed her eyes again. She could have sworn she'd heard Daniel saying her name. It must have been no more than a dream.

10

The next day Jim drove her home. 'Christine's dug out her old baby alarm,' he told her, 'and rigged it up in your flat. If you want anything, or if you feel ill at all, you've to get on to it and call down to the surgery. Someone'll come up.'

'Oh, I couldn't do that. You'll be busy.'

'Not too busy to attend to you if you need it. Not that I think you will,' he added, 'because you look in pretty good shape, all things considered. It would take more than an enraged bull to get the better of you.'

'Can't say I want to meet him again in a hurry though,' Keira conceded.

'I don't expect so. And it gave Frank Kelman quite a turn, too. He was as white as a sheet when Daniel turned up.'

Daniel?' Keira jerked upright in the seat, wincing as the movement brought a sharp pain to her temple. 'What did Daniel have to do with this?'

'Oh, he was the one they called out, didn't you know? As it happens he was out that way, doing house calls. He was at the Kelman's farm in five minutes flat, God knows what speed he must have been doing to get there that fast. We won't go into that. Anyway, he was first on the scene, and phoned for an ambulance to get you to A&E in Steadham. Insisted on going with you as well, and I reckon he would have stayed at your side if he hadn't got other patients to think about.'

'I see.' Keira thought back. So it was possible that she'd heard Daniel calling her name, maybe as she lay semi-conscious at the back of the bullpen. Her cheeks heated as she thought back. What had she mumbled in return?

Whatever it was it hadn't inspired Daniel to come to her side in the hospital. As a doctor he could surely have done that if he'd wanted. So plainly, having done his duty by her, he considered that was enough.

Christine was Keira's first visitor. She was carrying a bunch of late roses and a large fruit cake. 'The roses are from the garden,' she explained, 'but the fruit cake's from Mrs Grainger. She's out of hospital now and back with her beloved cats. She says to tell you that she would have come herself, but she doesn't think she could manage the stairs just yet. But the cats are fine, and — ' she paused meaningfully — 'she wondered if you might like a kitten. One of her moggies has just had a litter.'

'That'll be Sabrina,' Keira said with a smile. 'If the kittens take after her they'll be a very pretty bunch; she's a lovely cat. I'd love a kitten, though I don't know how it would cope with these stairs. Perhaps it's not such a good idea.'

'Well, think about it.' Christine produced a bulging carrier bag. 'Get well cards. You can look through them at your leisure. These have all been handed in at the surgery, plus a few that came by post. You really have a lot of well-wishers in the village, Keira.'

Keira said nothing. Her heart was full. She'd been at Acresfield Medical Centre for such a short space of time, and already all these people had taken her to their hearts. It was a very warming thought.

There was one question that she desperately wanted to ask, yet she was somehow afraid to do so. Fortunately, Christine seemed to sense what she wanted.

'Daniel sent round a box of fruit. I couldn't carry it up the stairs with all this lot, but Lianne will be up with it in a minute or two. A very doctorly present, don't you think? Plenty of vitamin C to help you recover.'

'That's very kind of him,' Keira said quietly.

It was kind, but she had to admit she would have traded a ton of fruit just for the sight of his face or the sound of his voice.

'Now you're signed off for a week,' Christine reminded her, 'so I don't want to see your face in the surgery before then. And you're only allowed back when you've had a thorough medical check. Understood?'

'Understood.' Keira gave in, it was pointless to do otherwise.

That evening she sat on the sofa with her feet up listening to the radio. Outside a light rain was falling and it was cold enough for her to appreciate the warmth of the gas fire. Its light and that of a small table lamp were the only illumination in the room; she found it restful.

She had almost decided to have an early night with a good book when there was a soft knock on the door. Probably Christine come to check up, she thought with a smile.

'Come in.'

The next moment she caught her breath. Her visitor was Daniel.

'Hi. I wondered how you were feeling.'

'I'm fine, thanks. I feel a fraud, getting all this time off.'

'You're anything but. That was a hefty blow you got from old Tyson.'

'So I hear.'

There was an awkward silence, then they both began to speak at once.

'Well, I'm glad to see — '

'I hope Finn is — '

They both started laughing, the ice broken. 'Oh, come in, and shut the door.' Keira invited. 'You're letting in a terrible draught. Would you like something to drink?'

She started to get up, but Daniel shook his head at her. 'You stay exactly where you are, doctor's orders. I'll make it, what would you like?'

'I'd love a hot chocolate, please. There's milk in the fridge and the chocolate powder is in the cupboard above it.'

'Right. I'll make myself a coffee while I'm at it.'

171

Daniel came back with two mugs on a tray. 'I found this packet of shortbread too. You have to keep your strength up.'

Keira laughed. 'Not much though! I'm hardly getting any exercise just sitting here. I can almost feel the pounds piling on.'

'You don't need to worry, believe me.' Daniel's eyes flicked appreciatively over her trim frame. 'When I saw you lying there after the accident, so white, so still, with that huge bruise on the side of your head. I can't explain how I felt.'

'You don't need to,' Keira said quietly. 'Because it's probably just the same as I felt when I saw you lying in the market square that first time I arrived in Penderby.'

'Tables turned.' Daniel grinned. 'The local paper has picked up on it already. They interviewed me for an article about it yesterday.'

'They're quick off the mark,' Keira commented.

'You held my hand tightly all the

way to the hospital.'

'I'm sorry.'

'Don't be. I was glad to be there.'

The only sound in the room was the slight hissing of the gas fire, and the rain pattering down the window.

'Daniel,' she began quietly. 'It's about Miriam — '

He looked up abruptly. 'You don't have to talk about her if you don't want to. I understand how you feel.'

'No, I don't think you do.' She cradled her mug, letting its warmth preface her fingers. 'You see, I had only ever heard her side of things. Never yours. That's my fault, I know; I never wanted to talk about it with you. But your friend, Peter, spoke to me about it. He didn't realise I was a friend of Miriam's. What he told me shocked me — and impressed me — very much.' She paused for breath. 'And I'm sorry, Daniel. I think I misjudged you.'

He said nothing, and Keira began to fear she'd done the wrong thing. Perhaps he simply wanted to forget about it, make a fresh start with Fiona.

He drained his coffee mug and put it down on the low table that separated them. 'How much did he tell you?' he asked at last.

Briefly Keira repeated the conversation she'd had with Peter on the night of the dance.

'So, he explained everything, did he?' Daniel asked when she'd finished.

'I think so, yes.'

'Not quite. He told you I was in love with someone else. He didn't say who that was.'

He was looking straight at her now, his direct gaze a challenge. Keira opened her mouth, but the words wouldn't come. The next moment there was a knock on the door, and Daniel stifled a muttered curse.

Jim Bishop came in, followed by Christine. 'Evenin' you two. Hope we're not breaking anything up?'

Daniel got to his feet. 'No, I was just leaving. Good night Keira, and thanks for the coffee. I'll be round again in the next few days.'

As the door shut behind him Jim sat down. 'Tell me the truth, did we interrupt anything' he asked worriedly. 'All this romantic atmosphere, the dim lighting — '

'That's just because bright light still hurts my eyes,' Keira said, not wanting him to feel uncomfortable.

'Well, Christine and I thought we'd come and see you before you went to bed. Christine's here in case you want any help in the shower or anything.'

'That's very thoughtful of you,' Keira said. She smiled and chatted, but inwardly she was wretched. If only they had come even five minutes later!

* * *

The next day there was no sign of Daniel, nor the day after that. Keira had plenty of other visitors, and the supply of cards and flowers continued unabated. She read the report of the

175

incident in the local press and wondered if Daniel was being teased about it as much as she'd been after the market-place incident.

The life of ease was beginning to pall. She'd read all the magazines kind people had brought, daytime TV failed to interest her, and thanks to Christine and Lianne there was no housework to be done in the neat, little flat. She opened the window and leaned out, admiring the autumn tints of leaves and inhaling the scent of woodsmoke in the air.

Then she stiffened. A man in a tracksuit was jogging up the lane, at his side a gangly, lolloping hound. Daniel and Finn.

Without thinking she pushed her arms into the sleeves of her jacket and hurried down the stairs. If she was quick she could just about intercept him.

Her legs felt unsteady, but she pushed herself on, running across the yard and into the lane. If she didn't get a move on he would have gone past, and then she'd never catch him up. Her heart was pounding, she felt dizzy. 'Daniel!' With her last reserves of energy she urged herself forward, emerging into the lane almost exactly as he came up to her, and collapsed into his arms.

He was very annoyed with her. 'What on earth do you think you're doing?'

He held her in his arms for a second, staring at her as if he couldn't believe what he was seeing. Then he scooped her up and set off back to the flat, Finn barking excitedly alongside. Upstairs he kicked open the door then gently put her down on the sofa, holding both her hands in his. 'How are you feeling?'

'Fine. Well, no, not so fine. Rather woozy, actually.'

'I'm not surprised, charging out at us like that.' He was taking her pulse, looking her over with a professional eye. 'Would you care to explain yourself?'

'I wanted so much to talk to you. I

saw you running down the lane with Finn, and I decided to go after you.'

Daniel gave her a mock-pitying smile. 'And what makes you think we weren't coming here in the first place?'

He was still holding her hands, even though there was no medical reason to do so. 'I stayed away for a couple of days because I felt we both needed some space. Then I decided to come round this afternoon and bring Finn. He's been missing you, too.'

'It's great to see him.' Keira leaned over and patted Finn's shaggy grey back. He woofed contently.

'We were interrupted the other night,' Daniel went on, I think I was on the point of revealing the name of the girl I'd fallen for back at university. That's what I want to do now.'

His eyes were very steady and full on hers, so that she could see herself reflected in the dark pupils. Her voice was unsteady. 'I think I know.'

'I think you do. It was you, Keira. I went to Africa to try to get you out of my mind. And I thought I had. But when you came to Penderby I realised I hadn't succeeded. Everything came flooding back.'

'I should have trusted my feelings about you, Keira said. 'But I accepted what Miriam said. Poor thing, I do hope she can manage to put the past behind her.'

'I hope so, too. Will you try to get back in touch with her?'

'Oh yes. I'm sure when she's calmed down I'll be able to talk to her — let her know I — we — still want her as a friend.'

'I'm glad you think that way,' Daniel said. 'I was pretty sure you'd want to try to cure Miriam of her fixation with the past. But you and I, we have the future to look forward to.'

He leaned forward and gently kissed her lips. 'The first thing we have to do is get you back on your feet.'

'I'm well on the way to recovery, thank you, Doctor,' Keira said, smiling up at him. 'But just one thing. What about Fiona? I hope she's not going to be hurt.'

Daniel shook his head. 'Not much danger of that. I don't meet her high standards, not a good enough horseman. It was good while it lasted, but we can part without regret. We'll still be good friends, and I think she'll warm to you once she knows you share her passion for horses.'

Keira grinned. 'As long as that's the only passion we share!'

She closed her eyes as their lips met once again, reminding herself to give Tyson the bull a pat on the back next time she saw him.

That kick from his mighty hoof had done more than propel her across the stall, it had sent her flying into a whole new life. One that held more than a promise of happiness.

SUMMER IN HANOVER SQUARE

Charlotte Grey

The impoverished Margaret Lambart is suddenly flung into all the glitter of the Season in Regency London. Suspected by her godmother's nephew, the influential Marquis St. George, of being merely a common adventuress, she has, nevertheless, a brilliant success, and attracts the attentions of the young Duke of Oxford. However, when the Marquis discovers that Margaret is far from wanting a husband he finds he has to revise his estimate of her true worth.

CONFLICT OF HEARTS

Gillian Kaye

Somerset, at the end of World War I: Daniel Holley, unhappily married to an ailing wife and father of four grown-up children, is attracted to beautiful schoolteacher Harriet Bray, but he knows his love is hopeless. Daniel's only daughter, Amy, who dreams of becoming a milliner and is caught up in her love for young bank clerk John Tottle, looks on as the drama of Daniel and Harriet's fate and happiness gradually unfolds.

THE SOLDIER'S WOMAN

Freda M. Long

When Lieutenant Alain d'Albert was deserted by his girlfriend, a replacement was at hand in the shape of Christina Calvi, whose yearning for respectability through marriage did not quite coincide with her profession as a soldier's woman. Christina's obsessive love for Alain was not returned. The handsome hussar married an heiress and banished the soldier's woman from his life. But Christina was unswerving in the pursuit of her dream and Alain found his resistance weakening . . .

THE TENDER DECEPTION

Laura Rose

When Sophia Barton was taken from Curton Workhouse to be a scullery-maid at Perriman Court, her future looked bleak. Was it really an act of Providence that persuaded Lady Perriman to adopt her as her ward? Sophia was brought up together with the Perriman children, and before sailing with his regiment for India, George, the heir to the title, declared his love. But tragedy hit the family and Sophia found herself caught up in a web of mystery and intrigue.